By the
Highway Home

Harper & Row, Publishers
New York, Evanston, San Francisco and London

By the Highway Home

Highway Home

by Mary Stolz

BY THE HIGHWAY HOME
Copyright © 1971 by Mary Stolz
All rights reserved. Printed in the United States of America. No part of thi
book may be used or reproduced in any manner whatsoever without writte
permission except in the case of brief quotations embodied in critical article
and reviews. For information address Harper & Row, Publishers, Inc., 10 Ea
53rd Street, New York, N.Y. 10022. Published simultaneously in Canada b
Fitzhenry & Whiteside Limited, Toronto.

Trade Standard Book Number 06-025830-6
Harpercrest Standard Book Number 06-025831-4

Library of Congress Catalog Number: 71-159046

Êste livro é para
Maria França e Bill e Johanna.

By the
Highway Home

Chapter 1

"What's Daddy doing out on the lawn with a flashlight?"

"Looking for your sister's night brace."

"I bet she lost it on purpose again."

"Oh, Catty."

Mrs. Reed turned from the window, through which she'd been watching her husband crawl around on his hands and knees patting the dry grass of their front yard. A streetlight down the way cast a hard illumination, and in any case it was not absolutely dark yet, but trying to find something as inconspicuous as Virginia's night brace would require luck as well as advantage.

Catty, reluctant to be considered small-minded — reluctant, indeed, to *be* small-minded — tried to mend her remark.

"Ginny is a beauty," she said. "Naturally she feels obliged to flirt, and it's hard to do with a rubber band going around your head and into both sides of your mouth. I mean, she can't even *smile* because of all that tinfoil or whatever it is. She coquettes by being mysterious, keeping her mouth closed and looking downward. Or sideways."

"I can't understand why you and your sister are so horrid to each other."

"I was trying not to be horrid. Anyway, were you and your sister so nice to each other when you were young?"

"As I remember it, yes. We were friends."

"Why didn't you stay friends?"

"Now, what do you mean by that?"

"Nothing. But you never write or anything. Or visit. It seems to me that if a couple of sisters were such good friends when they were kids then when they were grown up they'd — "

"Catty!"

"Okay. I was only saying."

Mrs. Reed exhaled a long breath. Like, thought Catty, someone who had just flopped on a bed and given up for the day. But apparently her mother had not given up because she decided to explain.

"Running that inn in Vermont is a more than full-time job. And we live here — almost a thousand miles away. We've never been letter-writers in my family, and we can't always be visiting."

"Always? We've only even seen her once, when she came here. We've never gone there," Catty pointed out.

4

"Not even on Daddy's vacation. I mean, you took Beau when he was little, but never the rest of us."

"Taking four — " Mrs. Reed stopped, drew a breath, " — three children halfway across the country is not, I'm afraid, our idea of holiday. I'm sorry. Besides, my sister and I do write to each other."

"At Christmas."

"Catty!"

"I was only saying that if — "

"Stop it! I have enough on my mind. He'll never find that thing out there."

"But I don't understand the flap. It's not expensive."

"We're not talking about the expense. Your father and I aren't anyway. Not about the night brace either, really. We're talking about larger things. Like standards of thoughtfulness, of responsibility, of — of respect!"

Thinking that all this might be better said, at the moment, to Ginny, Catty looked at the floor unspeaking.

"She says she took it off for a second, she *thinks* in the front yard. The cost of this orthodontia, and Ginger just takes an important part of it *off* for a second. It's enough to make a person scream."

"I'm glad I'm not going to get my teeth straightened. It looks terrible and it goes on forever and there's all this talk about money."

"There wouldn't be all this talk about money if a little proper care were taken."

"Mother, I haven't lost my night brace. It's Virginia, remember? I'm the one who isn't getting her teeth straightened."

"You'll be lucky to get anything to chew with them, leave alone have them straightened." Mrs. Reed had an expression her daughter had come to know, a sort of ironed-out look she got when she was saying something they weren't supposed to believe, and when she was saying something unpleasant they had to accept.

The trouble is, thought Catty, looking at her mother carefully, I get mixed up which time is which. On the whole, she had an uncomfortable idea that her mother was probably serious now.

Something was wrong, and, in the way of parents, they kept whatever it was from their children but let them pick it up in the air. The looks her mother and father exchanged when television newsmen talked about the nation's slumped economy, the rising cost of living, inflation, and the wage-price spiral. You heard of these from newspapers and teachers and, most of all, parents.

Nothing in this family had been the same since — Catty, even in her mind, had to pause — nothing had been the same since Beau had gone. The closeness, the laughter, had disappeared so much that Catty sometimes wondered how truly they had ever been there.

But now there was a different sense of trouble. A sharpness that wasn't sorrow. And there was talk about money all the time, all the time.

"I go into the market these days," Mrs. Reed would say, "with the same feeling I used to get if I opened my purse and found all the money gone. And no matter *how* much you spend, you get home with bags full of paper towels and deodorants. There's never anything to *eat* for all that money . . ."

"That's not actually true," Catty had pointed out once. "Now, in today's groceries — "

"Catty, stop picking," her mother had said, and Catty had stopped immediately, not persisting as she would once have done, so that she and her mother would have ended up either yelling at each other or laughing.

Now she said, "Here comes Daddy."

Mr. Reed opened the front screen door, let it bang behind him, and came into the living room dangling a wide rubber band with silver hooks at each end.

"Isn't that wonderful, Jim," said his wife. "You actually found it."

"Get Virginia down here," Mr. Reed said to Catty, who looked at him in surprise, then rushed away up the stairs. Her father was almost never like that, even these days. Practically rude. The loss of the night brace must be more serious than she thought.

But the thing didn't cost much, and anyway Ginny was finishing up next month with the whole tooth scene, so why were their parents so exercised, so overwrought?

Standards of thoughtfulness, of responsibility, of respect. Oh, murder. She knocked softly on the door of the room she and her sister shared, and wondered as she waited what it *had* cost, exactly, to make Ginger's smile look perfect to go along with the perfect-looking rest of her.

Ginger, nearly sixteen, made it clear that even if they two had to be confined in a room together, certain formalities were to be observed. One of them was knocking when the door was closed. Which would be fine, Catty thought, if she knocked when I close the door. When she'd pointed this out one day, Ginger had said kids of thirteen didn't need privacy.

"You know something," Catty replied. "You don't have nice feelings. Maybe that's why nobody likes you."

Ginger had slapped her face, and then burst into tears and begged Catty not to tell on her. From time to time Ginny had slapped, pinched, and even bitten her younger sister and brother, but Catty and Lex never did tell on her. Lexy, Catty assumed, because he was so good-natured. Or maybe he figured Ginger had a right to push him around a bit, since he was only eight. And she always apologized so furiously after she'd done something mean that Lexy, easily moved by other people's emotions, though reserved about his own, probably felt sorry for her.

And Catty didn't tell because she wouldn't admit to anyone that her sister was a bully. Besides, if you had to be honest, and sometimes, for the sake of self-respect, you had to try to be — she said some pretty gross things to Ginny. That about nobody liking her, for instance. That was cutting. And not entirely true. Almost, but not entirely.

She opened the door.

Virginia was sitting in front of the mirror, an arm crooked behind her head, long auburn hair streaming sideways (arranged to do so), closed lips smiling dreamily, eyes mischievously glancing at her reflection . . . *Adorable, oh you adorable thing . . .*

At Catty's entrance she jerked around. "Why do you always come in here without knocking?"

"I knocked. I *never* come in without knocking."

"I did not hear you."

"No wonder. Such total self-absorption probably blocks the eustachian tubes."

"Oh, for heaven's sake. Look, save your snippets of half-knowledge for people who'll be impressed by them. That's a completely unscientific thing to say and you don't even know what a eustachian tube is."

"I know what self-absorption is."

Ginger clenched her fists. "Oh . . . oh . . . oh! Oh, *why* did I have to be born into this family? All the families in the world and this is the one *I* get stuck with!"

"Mom and Daddy would just love to hear you say that."

"I don't mean them. What do you want anyway? Go away."

"Daddy found your night brace. He sounds sort of cross to me. He's been crawling around in the garden looking for it for ages."

"Garden! Two bushes and a sunflower."

"Okay . . . yard. Daddy wants to talk to you. The least you could've done was help him look."

"I did help, until it got dark. Nobody could find that thing in the dark."

"He did find it. I think you'd better get down there, if you've finished gazing at yourself."

"And I think I'd sell my chances at immortality for a room of my own."

"I'd like one, too," Catty was forced to say, but thought a bit wryly that she'd probably, in that case, have to leave a light burning all night because of her

9

unconquerable fear of the dark. "Did you know Virginia Woolf wrote a book called that? *A Room of One's Own*."

"Of course. Virginia Woolf was a precursor of the Woman's Lib Movement," Ginger began and then remembered she was annoyed. "You're much too young to understand Virginia Woolf."

"According to you I'm much too young to understand anything, but do give me leave to try."

Virginia pushed past her and went downstairs. Catty hesitated, decided not to follow. She disliked talks where their parents tried to reason with them and they tried to resist being reasonable. Because even when they had right on their side — which they frequently did — you got this feeling of grown-up people just having their way because they were grown up.

Daddy even said it once in a while, when one of them had exasperated him beyond the point he was willing to endure. "Why?" he'd say. "Because I'm bigger than you are and I say so, that's why."

He could make it sound funny, loving, even laughing-at-himself, but the fact stayed. He could make you do something, or keep you from doing it, because he was bigger and older than you were.

When I grow up, thought Catty, who was small for her age, I'll always remember what it was like, feeling reduced by other people's size. It was this smallness in Lexy that made her love him. Or partly. Lex was awfully easy to love. Even Ginger seemed to love him, when she could get her mind off herself.

Catty went down the hall to her brother's room and opened the door cautiously. It was past his bedtime, but he might just be awake in the dark and talking to himself. No, sound asleep. A slender form under the blankets that she could just make out by the glow of the nightlight. She pulled the door softly and went to the head of the stairs.

Her father was talking, sounding tired.

"Virginia, I am not saying that the night brace itself costs much. I'm saying that with the cost of getting your teeth straightened, the least we can expect is that you do your part."

"That thing hurts. It feels as if it were breaking my neck."

"Then let's stop the whole business! Two years of it, and eighteen hundred dollars so far, and six of these damn night harnesses lost, and I'm fed up!"

Silence, and then Ginger, in a small voice, "I'm sorry, Daddy. I won't lose them anymore."

"You'd better not. And wear them when you're supposed to, do you understand? One more episode like this and the deal's off. You can grow fangs for all I care."

Catty, at the top of the stairs, arms around her knees, stared toward the voices and wondered what was wrong with their father. What was really wrong?

If I were Mother, she thought, I'd remind him that the deal's off next month anyway. Two years and eighteen hundred dollars and a month from now Virginia, debraced, will go forth to dazzle all beholders. Huh.

But Mrs. Reed said nothing, and Catty got up and went to get ready for bed.

Chapter 2

Her teachers, the principal, the school nurse and a few of her parent's friends called her Catherine. To everyone else she was Catty. As happens with people who have nicknames, she was asked how it had come about.

"I mean," said a girl at school, "does it mean you're *catty*? Or batty over catties?"

"Bats about cats."

"Me, too. How many do you have?"

"None."

"Well, but why ever not?"

"My brother, Beau, is allergic to them. His eyes itch and his nose stuffs up whenever he's near a cat. They give him asthma."

"What tough luck."

"Oh, if he's careful he's all right."

"No, I meant that you can't have a *cat*."

There had been the time when she and Lexy had sneaked a kitten into the house, thinking that what Beau didn't know wouldn't give him asthma. They got a pan and put torn up newspapers in it and planned to keep the kitten in Lexy's room until Beau, having spent several days in the same house with a cat, would have to admit that he only got allergic if he knew the cat was there.

That evening, Beau, who'd been sixteen at the time, got in from his part-time job at a gas station, where he worked after school and on weekends, and suddenly began to sneeze.

"What the heck," he said, blowing hugely on his handkerchief. "What's this all about? I must be catching a cold."

Catty and Lex had looked at each other nervously, not speaking. Beau had gone on sneezing, and then began to wheeze.

"I can't understand it," he said miserably, breathing through his mouth. "Ma, you don't think I'm going to start getting this over nothing, do you? I can try to stay away from cats all right, but if I'm going to start doing this when there isn't even a cat in — "

Catty jumped up and threw her arms around her adorable, sneezing, wheezing brother.

"Beau," she cried, "I'm sorry. We're sorry, Lex and me — "

13

"Sure, sure, Cats. I know you are. I just — I just — "
He sneezed violently.

"No, you don't understand. There *is* a cat in the place.
I mean, it's just a kitten. Lex and I found it, a dog had
chased it into a tree, but we thought if you didn't know
it was here — " She stopped, sighing, and looked at her
mother. "We're sorry."

"Well," said Mrs. Reed, "we'll have to get it out, right
now."

"Yeah, but wait a sec," said Beau. "We just can't toss
it out the door, now it thinks it's been adopted."

Beau held no grudge against cats for putting him in
this condition. He said it was too bad it wasn't three-toed
sloths that gave him the wheezes, because he could do
without them handily but would have liked having a cat
around the house. Catty thought he'd have managed,
given the chance, to like a three-toed sloth in residence.

Where Beau was concerned, animals had first rights
over human beings, even though they couldn't assert
them. Probably because they couldn't assert them.

"If you're so into pets," someone had asked him once,
"why no dog? You aren't allergic to them."

"I'm not into *pets*," Beau had explained patiently.
"And dogs seem to be in some basic confusion about
their role. Are they creatures, or some sort of human
beings? I like animal animals, and especially I like them
on their own, living where they're supposed to live. Safe
from us. Not that they ever can be."

"Phone some of your friends," he said now to Catty.
"Maybe you can find someone to take it."

Catty found all her friends willing to take the kitten and none of their mothers willing. "I don't understand," she moaned. "It's such a pretty little kitten, Beau. Black and white, like a tiny skunk."

"Nonetheless," Mrs. Reed said firmly. "It must go. Now. Beau is getting worse by the second. Hop upstairs and get it and take it out to the car. We'll just have to drive over to the Humane Society with it."

"But suppose they want to put it to sleep? That's what happened to the cat Amy Gruber found. They said there were too many homeless cats as it is and the kindest thing to do is put them away. *I* don't think that's kind."

"It may be kinder," Mrs. Reed said, "than letting it go hungry and homeless and — "

Lexy set up a howl of despair. "I don't want our kitty put to sleep!"

"Do you want your brother to choke to death?"

"No, no," wailed Lexy. "No, I don't. I want — I dunno *what* I want." And he, too, blew his nose with a honking sound and began to gasp and cry.

Into this scene came Mr. Reed, who stared around and asked what the deuce was going on.

"Beau's getting asthma, because the children sneaked a cat into the house and — "

"They didn't really sneak it," Beau began, but Mr. Reed interrupted.

"How could you do a thing like that?" he demanded of Catty. "You know what cats do to Beau."

"Daddy, we thought if he didn't know it was here, he wouldn't *get* allergic," Catty said, and began to cry. "It's not a cat, it's just a little kitten," she sobbed. "I wouldn't hurt *Beau*."

"This is preposterous." Mr. Reed looked at his three children as their eyes streamed and their breath shuddered. "Get the thing — I mean, the cat — the kitten — and take it out to the car. I'll drive over to the Humane Society with it."

"Yeah, but Dad," said Beau, "that's what the bellowing is about. The kids are afraid they'll put the kitten to sleep."

"Maybe we can get someone to take it."

"We've tried everyone we can think of," said his wife. "No one wants it. Now Catty and Lex, go up and get it, *please*."

Driving to the Humane Society with her father (Lexy had refused to come), Catty held the kitten against her chest, crooning to it. "Don't be scared, darling," she said softly. "Don't be frightened."

Far from being frightened, the kitten purred as she licked Catty's chin. She was alert and homely, with, Mr. Reed said glumly, so much personality that it came across even in this short ride. By the time they got to the Humane Society, he was looking thoughtful.

"Is there any way," he asked a young man who came into the office when they entered, "to save it? Such a fine little creature, so full of life and sass. Be a pity to— Catty, don't start crying again."

"Well now, let's see," said the attendant, taking the kitten gently up and examining her. He put her on the counter, rubbed her ears and shook his head. "Female.

We can't let females out for adoption. I'm sorry, little girl. But try to see that it's best this way. A female kitten will grow into a cat and have litters and you never know what their lives will be. People don't take the care of cats that they do of dogs. The poor things could starve or freeze if no one wants them. You'd hate that, wouldn't you?"

The kitten had found a rubber band and flicked it far enough down the counter to be worth stalking. Flattening to her belly, legs angled upward, she moved cautiously, setting one front foot before the other with delicate precision, wobbling only slightly, great eyes fixed and staring, tail tip vibrating. Within inches of the prey, she adandoned stealth, sprang into the air and pounced on her prize. Carefree and frivolous, oblivious to Fate, she lay on her side holding the rubber band close with her front paws and shoving it away with her hind feet.

"Oh, *Daddy!*"

"Why can't you keep it yourselves, since you like it so much?" the attendant asked, and clucked unhappily when the situation was explained. "Only out," he said hesitantly, "would be for you to pay for her to be spayed. We can nearly always arrange adoption for a spayed female. Then people don't have to worry about litters and prowling toms, you know."

"What does that cost?" Mr. Reed asked.

"Twenty-five bucks, I'm afraid."

Before her father could speak, Catty said excitedly, "Lex and I will give you our allowance. I mean, I know

I will and I'm sure he will, and I bet Beau would help, too. Please, Daddy. Please — I mean, *look* at her!"

So the kitten, unaware that she owed her life to three young people who never saw her again, was taken a week later by an old woman who loved her on sight and took her home to the best of everything and a longer life than Beau had.

When Beau, two years later, ran off to join the Marines, Lexy suggested that maybe now they could have a kitten of their own, but even Catty had rejected this. Beau would be coming home to see them on his holidays, or leaves, or whatever they were called—Catty, the word lover, was too miserable to straighten out military terminology. Beau would be coming home for good one day when he'd paid for being, as Mr. Reed put it, "a hare-brained fool," and when Beau came home he was not going to get asthma. He was going to find his house as he'd left it.

When Beau, "Proving," Mr. Reed said in a harsh and strangling voice, "that he was not a coward," had died in Vietnam last November, no one had said that now they would be free to have a cat whenever they wished. Months later, when the corroding pain that she had known would never lessen had, in fact, lessened, Catty considered owning a kitten. The thought that she could think it, that she could want anything now that Beau was gone, caused her anguish that was just bearable and quite unshareable.

That was when she had begun to lie looking into the dark, night after night. When she did fall asleep there were nearly always nightmares waiting for her. Sometimes it seemed that nothing could make her believe Beau was gone. All those billions and billions of people in the world, and not one of them was Beau anymore. It was not possible, and she could not accept it.

But other times she knew he was dead, and those were the worst times of all.

Chapter 3

"Ginger," said Catty from her bed, "do you think something's going on that Mom and Daddy aren't telling us?"

Virginia, smoothing body lotion on her legs with long indolent strokes, didn't reply. Her eyes had an inward, thoughtful expression, as if she found what she was thinking more interesting than what she was hearing. More often than not she gave that impression.

"Ginny!"

"What *is* it, Catty?"

"I said, do you get the feeling that something's wrong?"

Ginger, night brace in place, got into bed with her European history text. Catty was holding a volume of Hans Christian Andersen. She was rereading *The Little Mermaid* and getting ready to cry because it was toward the end, but somehow thoughts of her father and mother kept intruding.

"Wrong how?" Virginia said at last.

"I don't know how. Whatever wrong *means*. Awry, sinister, fateful, foreboding, ominous, prophetic, dire — "

"Yes, dear. You know heaps of words. Now, if you don't mind — "

"Daddy's cross as sticks and Mom keeps stopping what she's doing to stare."

"At what?"

"How should I know at what? She just stares, that's all." Ginger didn't respond, and after a moment, Catty went on, "I think she's thinking of Beau."

"Don't."

"I can't ever talk about him?"

"Not yet. Some day. Not now."

"But — "

"Catty, stop. You make people suffer, always wanting to talk about Beau. Don't you see that Mom and Dad and I *can't* talk about him yet? You're too young to know how we feel."

Catty picked up her book and pretended to read, but the words swam, and presently tears fell down her cheeks.

Her sister glanced over. "That *The Little Mermaid* again?"

Catty nodded.

"Why don't you read something cheery? I'm beginning to think you like to suffer. And *must* you chew your hair?"

Without a word, Catty turned on her side and pulled

the pillow over her head, a strand of straight brown hair in the corner of her mouth. She lay quietly, staring around the room, wishing Virginia would say something comforting, something nice. She wouldn't, of course. She didn't. She closed her book, turned out the light between their beds, and settled for sleep without even saying good-night.

" 'Night, Ginny," Catty whispered, telling herself that everything would be all right if her sister heard and said, " 'Night, Catty. Sleep well."

There was silence from the other bed, and presently Virginia's even breathing.

Catty turned the pillow, put it under her head, twisting restlessly. She tried to put herself to sleep with words. *Megalomaniac.* Do you know what a megalomaniac is? she asked her sleeping sister. Well, it's someone with delusions of personal grandeur. Some people have personal grandeur and some people have delusions of it. You're the deluded type. Do you know what a martyr is? Somebody who has to live with a megalomaniac. That's you and me. The megalomaniac and the martyr. But Virginia, if she'd been awake and paying attention, would only have said, "Which is which?"

Catty felt in her pajama pocket for a tissue, sniffled deeply when she found none, at length got up and went down the hall to the bathroom. When she came out, blowing her nose, her father was on the landing, a letter in his hand.

He looked at her closely. "Catty you've been crying."

"It's *The Little Mermaid,*" she gulped. "It always

makes me — " Suddenly she flung herself against him. "It isn't that, Daddy. It's — it's — I'm — "

"Now, now," he said gently, patting her back. "Tell H.D. what the trouble is."

She had to smile a little. When their father traveled he sent cards addressed to D.D.'s and S.S.'s, and signed them H.D. Catty couldn't remember when it had begun but it'd gone on for years, until Beau died. Now he'd have to say just S.S., so Catty figured that was why he didn't write cards like that anymore. Actually, he didn't travel much anymore. Or at all. When was the last time their father had taken a business trip?

"Dutiful Daughters and Serious Sons," he'd write. "Hot on trail of Questing Beast, sighted in thick thicket behind Sears, Roebuck outlet. Home with fewmets next Mon. Signed, Handsome Daddy."

Except he always used initials. Once one of Catty's friends had seen such a card on the living-room table and had frowned over it.

"What the heck does that mean?" she'd asked. "D.D.'s and S.S.'s and H.D. What *is* it?"

"Nothing, to you. But a lot to us," Catty had replied.

This was the first time in over a year she'd heard her father call himself H.D., and it was better than having Virginia hear her whispered good-night and reply it.

Catty believed in signs and omens, and at this one she wrapped her arms around her father's waist and set to crying in earnest.

"Well, well. We'll have to get to the bottom of this." Holding her close, he led her down the stairs and into the living room, where Mrs. Reed looked up in alarm.

"Catty," she said, jumping up. "Darling, what's wrong?"

"That's what I want to know!" Catty cried.

"And that's what we're going to find out," said Mr. Reed, depositing his daughter on the sofa. "Now, tell us," he directed. "Here." He handed her his big handkerchief. "A good blow, and then the tale, okay?"

Only now she didn't know where to start. What was she crying for? For her brother, Beau, killed in Indochina last fall and buried in the churchyard here in town in the rain one day in November? Beau, that only Lexy would let her talk about? Crying because her mother had taken to staring into space and not hearing when you asked her things? Because her father didn't write to them anymore when he traveled — or did he ever travel? — or call himself Handsome Daddy, or ever laugh? Crying because everything seemed sad and skimpy these days? Because her mother and father, who never used to fight with each other the way some people's parents did, had taken to having quiet hard-voiced arguments when they thought no one was around to hear?

Why *was* she crying, so that her throat and her chest felt lumpy and breathing seemed to choke her?

"Nobody — nobody is *happy* anymore," she said finally, gasping. "It's all so sad, since Beau —" She broke off, folded her lips, then shrieked, "Nobody lets me talk about Beau!"

Mrs. Reed put her arms around her daughter, who continued to cry for a long time but at length grew quiet and leaned her head against her mother's shoulder in a defeated gesture.

"I guess we've been wrong," Mr. Reed began slowly. "I guess we thought that if — if you children were given time — if we didn't refer to him too often — I don't know what we thought. Not that you'd forget, Catty. Just, perhaps, that you'd have time to heal. If we talk about him all the time — "

"Not all the time." Catty sighed. "Just sometimes. It's — This way, it's as if everybody wanted to forget him. I don't forget him. I think about him and think about him, but only Lex lets me say anything, and I think Lexy doesn't really understand that he's — that Beau is gone. Beau is dead. I don't know what Lexy thinks, but he talks as if Beau had gone around the corner for an hour. And that's nice. I mean, it's nice for me. Only I want you and Mom, and even Virginia, to act sometime as if you *remembered* him!"

"Remembered him?" said Mrs. Reed. "Act as if we remember Beau?"

Catty twisted painfully. "I didn't mean that. I mean — maybe act as if we hadn't *forgot* him. I don't know what I mean. Except we're never happy anymore. And I guess," she said, wretchedly truthful, "that I want to be happy. Even without him. I want to pretend he's gone around the corner for an hour and talk about him and forget him sometimes — " She pulled out of her mother's arms and leaned her head back, closing her eyes. "I'm not nice, am I?" she said sadly.

"Catty," said her father. "Open your eyes. Come on, look at me. That's better. Now — you are nice. See? In my opinion, you're one of the nicest cats around."

A smile quirked again at her lips.

"Your mother and I have apparently gone about trying to do the right thing in the wrong way, and we're sorry. And of course you want to be happy. So do we, and so do your sister and brother. Because we're nice normal human beings and that sort wants to be happy, no matter what. So don't get the idea that wanting to live happily means you're shutting Beau out. You — we — could never shut him out. And from now on, when you want to talk about him — " Mr. Reed broke off, breathing deeply, and then went on " — as if he'd gone around the corner for an hour, then do it, Catty. We'll all try. All right?"

Catty nodded, and now that she had permission, found she couldn't even say Beau's name again. She was tired, but didn't want to go upstairs yet, and her parents just sat there, her father in the chair close to them, her mother beside her, very quiet.

"What's that?" she asked, looking at the letter her father had dropped on the table when he brought her downstairs.

Mr. and Mrs. Reed looked at each other, then at their exhausted, tear-stained daughter who was still too overwrought for sleep.

"A letter from my sister," Mrs. Reed said. Catty caught her lower lip. "That's all right," said Mrs. Reed, guessing, as she often did, what was in another person's mind. "You had no way of knowing Marian and I have been writing to each other recently. I didn't tell you because — because your father and I haven't decided yet — " Her voice slowed, then speeded up. "Haven't decided what to tell any of you. Or how, maybe. Maybe how to tell you is what I mean."

Catty looked from her father to her mother and felt her stomach contract. I knew something was wrong, she thought. I knew it. I knew that something besides Beau was making them cross and sad.

"I think," she said, "that when something is wrong in a family, people are supposed to share."

"Why do you conclude something is wrong?" Mr. Reed asked, as his wife said, "You're only thirteen, Catty."

"Old enough to share. Especially when if you don't share, you get nervous and wondering all the time. Have you told Ginny?" she asked suddenly.

"Oh, Catty, no. No, we've been trying to figure a way to tell all of you."

"Tell us what?" Catty shouted, and looked up to see Virginia in the doorway.

"Yes," said Virginia, mumbling through the constriction of the night brace. "Yes, I'd like to know, too. We've been acting like a bunch of canaries with a cat on top of the cage, and it's been this way for ages. For once I'm on Catty's side, and I want to know what's going on."

"Your father's lost his job," Mrs. Reed said, throwing out the words the way you'd throw a plate on the floor, meaning to smash it. "You wanted to know. Now you know."

Virginia pulled off the night brace in order to speak her outrage and disbelief clearly. "You mean he doesn't have a job anymore?"

"I believe that's what I just said."

"But how — what did you *do*, Daddy?"

"He didn't *do* anything. There's a depression going on in this country that we're supposed to call a recession but it comes to people losing jobs who haven't *done* anything but work hard all their lives and — "

Mr. Reed put his hand over his wife's, and she grew quiet, but her breathing was quick and apparent.

Catty wondered whether to start crying again, this time because she was frightened, but decided against it. She'd told them that thirteen was old enough to share. Sorry that she'd asked, wishing she'd stayed in the ignorance of grown-up problems that being thirteen should entitle her to, she pushed her shoulders back against the sofa and tried to look alert.

She was tired. Daddy would find another job. He'd have to, because if he didn't what would happen to them? But why did she have to listen to them talking about it? She wished she were Lexy's age, asleep like Lexy. She wished that she'd gone to sleep tonight and not met her father in the hall or not asked them to tell her anything or talk about Beau. She wished she'd kept Beau in her mind, in her heart, and let Daddy and Mom work out what to do about being fired and *then* share the trouble when it was all over and settled.

Fiercely she kept her eyes open, moving from her father's face to her mother's, as they explained how people at his plant were being laid off because of the slowdown in the national economy. Or because of something.

Drowzily she watched her father pick the letter up from the table, fumble for his glasses, and get them on.

"Marian," he began, "your mother's sister, has been proposed to by a — "

"A proposal of marriage?" Virginia said in surprise. "At her age?"

Mr. and Mrs. Reed looked at her helplessly.

"It's girls like you who drive other women into the Lib movement," said Mrs. Reed.

"What's that supposed to mean?"

"It means that for someone brought up in what we hoped was a fairly forward-looking manner, you have totally antebellum ideas. And I'm not sure which bellum I mean, either."

"Well, but after all, she must be practically forty, and if a woman hasn't got a man by the time she's — "

"Knock it off, Virginia," said her father. "You depress me. Do you two wish to hear any more?"

"I do," Catty offered, not meaning it.

"As I was saying, Marian is going to be married, and she and her husband will live in California. And so — " He stopped, coughed in the manner of one delaying an announcement, sighed and continued. "And so we — your mother and I — have decided — "

"Your great-uncle Henry will really need help running his inn, with Marian gone," Mrs. Reed said when her husband handed her the letter with a dispirited shrug. She began to read. "Dearest Amy — How in the world can I bring you up to date? Well, to begin with, Amy, I am in love — "

Catty was asleep.

Chapter 4

After Beau was killed, Catty had begun to have nightmares. She was also afraid of things in the day, although
when Ginny asked her impatiently *what* things, Catty
couldn't say.

Of sirens, storms, bus drivers, closets, parties, strangers, some girls, all boys. But it wasn't really any of
those. Of being alone? But she had always liked to be
alone.

She was not sure what frightened her, but she refused
to go to school if Virginia didn't walk with her, and
walk back with her. Catty's school lay on the way to
Ginny's, and both were close enough to walk to except
on very rainy mornings.

And so, every school morning, a fast moving and
usually impatient Virginia was accompanied by her

younger sister, and every afternoon Virginia had to stop at Catty's school and walk her home.

"It's like having a *trailer* attached to me," Ginger complained to her parents.

"Don't be unkind, Ginny," Mrs. Reed would say. "It isn't like you."

Which shows all parents know about things, Catty would think. Ginny could be unkind, all right. She could be mean. She could, of course, sometimes be sort of nice.

This morning she stood in the doorway, saying, "Catty, if you're coming, will you please get with it. I want to be in school early, and I won't wait."

She was already dressed, in a bright red thing that somehow looked wonderful with her dark red hair. Virginia, even with braces gleaming across her smile like silver foil, was a pretty, a very pretty, girl. Lots of people said she was beautiful, but they didn't have to share a room with her.

Catty sat on her tumbled bed, pulling on socks, hearing her sister's voice in the distance. She usually fell asleep so late that mornings were unreal, and she moved into wakefulness slowly, feeling her way.

They had breakfast in their nightclothes, on the theory that food would jostle Catty and get her going, but after Virginia and Lexy had finished eating and gone to make their beds, Catty would be apt still to be staring into her cereal bowl like a half-awake fortune-teller.

At length she'd finish and go back upstairs to dress.

Her bed she left until afternoon, and Ginny had given up protesting.

"All I ask," she'd say, "is that somehow she get into her clothes and out the door so we can get to school before the day's half over. It'll be a miracle if I get an education, that's all I have to say."

It isn't all you have to say, Catty would think languidly. Nothing is ever all you have to say. You *always* have something more to say.

Catty, herself, was mute in the morning. Enough to get unfolded from wrappings and wrappings of sleep. She sometimes thought of it as yards and yards and yards of some soft warm stuff that got layered around her loosely, lightly, cloudily.

But in her nightmare nights, sleep seemed like the stiff clay-colored shredding strips that encased Egyptian mummies at the museum and then, often as not, she'd wake up screaming.

"Now listen," said Ginger, tapping her foot. "I'm going to count to ten, and if you aren't ready, I'm leaving."

Stung into action, Catty grabbed a skirt from its hanger and struggled into it. "Count to fifty, please?" she begged.

In the way she had of suddenly turning nice, Ginny laughed and said, "All right. A hundred, if you positively need it. But honestly, I do want to get there early this morning, Catty. I have an experiment going in the chemistry lab."

Virginia might not be the most lovable party in Indiana, but Catty was pretty sure she was one of the smartest. At school work.

"Where's my sweater?" she mumbled. "Had it a minute ago."

Virginia pulled it out from under the pillow. "There. Now hurry."

They went into the kitchen to say good-bye to their mother, Catty looking around for their father. "Where's Daddy?"

"Looking for work. What he's done every day for a month now."

"But you said last night we were going to Vermont." Catty thought that over. "Didn't you?"

"Your father has this one more interview," Mrs. Reed said in a smooth forbidding voice. "Then we'll decide. You girls look nice. Catty, you've lost the button from your sweater."

"It's the bottom one."

"The bottom one doesn't count?"

"Not as much as in the middle."

"Catty, come *on*."

In the street, running to keep up, Catty said, "Did I go to sleep last night?"

"Yes."

"How did I get to bed?"

"Daddy carried you. I think you were rude, falling asleep in the middle of their explanation that *you* asked for."

"I was tired. What was the explanation, Ginny?"

"I guess we're moving to Vermont," Virginia said bitterly. "At least, that's how it sounded last night.

Aunt Marian's letter was all about moving there and helping Uncle Henry run his dreary inn."

"She said it was dreary?"

"I say it's dreary. I *hope* Daddy gets that job today. I don't want to move someplace where we won't know anybody, and I won't have any friends, and I don't care what *you* say, Catherine Reed, I do have friends and people do like me." Ginger sounded close to tears herself, and that was so unusual that Catty took fright.

"I didn't mean that, Ginny. It was just — I was angry." She couldn't remember now at what. "I'm sorry."

"Oh, forget it. What difference does it make? What difference does anything make now? You'd think a man could at least hold a job . . ."

"Don't you talk about Daddy that way, Virginia. Don't you — "

"In *case* you're interested," Ginger said in a cold tone, "you just passed your school." She walked rapidly away.

"Ginny! Don't forget to pick me up this afternoon!"

"What'll you do if I do forget, call the cops?" Virginia said over her shoulder. "Oh, don't look so stricken. I'll be here."

She was gone. Catty walked slowly into her school building. She should have more pride. But then, pride was where you found it, and if in its place you found fear —

Her first period teacher called her twice and then asked her to stop woolgathering.

"That's a good word," Catty said. "I wonder what the origins are?"

"It used to mean just what it says — shepherds went around gathering up tufts and tresses of wool that had got caught on bushes and briers as the sheep moved about grazing. These days we use it to describe people who get caught up in their dreams and fancies and ignore what's going on around them."

It was the only thing Catty learned in school that day, but she found it a pleasant piece of information.

Mr. Reed did not get the job. In the evening he told his family that as soon as they could sell the house they'd leave for Vermont. "And I think we should look on the move as a challenge," he said without assurance.

"Last night," Virginia said grimly, "you said that if we went we'd all be expected to help. What does that mean?"

"It means that Uncle Henry runs a family business and we're part of the family, so — "

"I don't feel part of Uncle Henry's family. I've never laid eyes on him, and neither have Lex or Catty."

"Virginia," her father said ominously, "you had better mind your words, and your behavior. I am pushed about to my limit. One more shove and I won't be responsible for how I act toward you. You're selfish and self-serving and in the ordinary course of things you'd continue to get away with it, but it happens that if we plan to go on eating and keeping a roof over our heads we'll have to grab this opportunity and be grateful it's there for the grabbing. You do not seem to understand the seriousness of our position. I know at least two men — good, hard-working men, who've done their damnedest

— who now have their families on relief. So you, Virginia, shut up. Do I make myself clear?"

"Perfectly." Virginia got to her feet. "You can't hold a job, so I have to go to work being a waitress, probably. What could be clearer?" She walked out of the room and up the stairs.

Mr. Reed turned a fatigue-lined face toward his wife. "I thought you told me that when the chips were down we'd all pull together?"

"Oh, Jim. Don't mind her. She's frightened, that's all. Ginny is one of those people who turn surly when they're alarmed."

"Like Pete Gormley's dog," Lexy offered. "Whenever Archie — that's Pete's dog — whenever Archie is scared he growls and tries to bite somebody. He only *tries* biting, of course, because he's scared to bite, too, so he doesn't, if you get what I mean."

"Well," said Catty, "I suppose Ginny's mad, all right, but I think it's going to be fun. I like doing different things."

"Me, too," said Lexy.

"It's my idea," Mrs. Reed said, "that no man should work at one job, or even one sort of job, his whole life long. This may be a gorgeous new beginning that we'll all love and that we would never have thought of if you hadn't lost the old job."

"What a bunch of Do-Goody Two-Shoes," said Mr. Reed, shaking his head. "Marvelous, all of you. What's for dinner?"

He's like me, Catty thought. He's changing the subject because he's filled with tenderness inside and he doesn't want it to show too much. I love you, she thought, looking at her father and thinking that maybe Beau would have looked like this one day, if he'd made it to forty-three. Dear and handsome and tired and sort of — used up. Her father would get old, but Beau never would. That should be a sort of comfort to consider. But it wasn't.

Chapter 5

The night before the moving men were to come for their things, the house caught on fire.

The first Catty and Ginger knew about it was when their mother came into their room and said in a low urgent voice, "Girls, girls, wake up. You, too, Catty. No nonsense about it. We have to get out. Now."

Ginger was on her feet in a second, but Catty tried to burrow back toward sleep.

She felt her mother's hand shaking her roughly, heard her say, "Catty, I'm telling you to get up now, this minute!"

"What's going on?" Ginger asked. "What's that smell?"

"There's a fire in the basement, and your father thinks we should get out of the house. Now, put on some clothes but don't stop to pack anything or save anything, do you understand? And hurry!"

Catty's swirl of sleepiness disappeared like a fog patch. She was dressed as quickly as Ginger, and down the hall to Lexy's room, where the door stood open.

"Lexy," she called. "Lex, where are you?"

"He's here with us," her father shouted. There was an acrid smell now and the hall was beginning to fill with smoke, so that Catty could scarcely make out the figures of her family at the head of the stairs.

Ginger, she noticed, was carrying her Keeping Box, a fairly large affair to which Catty had the mate, and in which they kept things of value. Beau's letters, his bronze cross, all her pictures of him were in her box. She headed back toward the bedroom and was brought up short by a bark from her father.

"Catty! Come back here this instant. We're getting out now!"

"But — "

"No buts, no anything. Come." He started for the stairs, fell back, hesitated, then turned and led the way to Lexy's room. "Now look, children. Everybody be calm. Just do what I say and we'll be fine. I'm going to get out on the roof outside Lex's room and you're all to follow me. I'll drop down to the ground and your mother will help you over the side and I'll catch you. That's clear?"

As he talked they'd all crowded into Lexy's room. Mr. Reed shut the door behind them, pushed up the screen and was out the window onto the porch.

Catty wondered if she were now frightened into

40

imagining heat and smoke rolling and lifting at them from downstairs, or whether this really was a last minute escape. Her heart was thudding so that it seemed to shake her whole body. Out in the night there were sirens and loud excited voices and shouts. Probably everybody in the street was there to watch their house burn, like in a movie about a fire.

Crawling out after Lexy, she watched as her mother, lying down, held her brother's thin arms and lowered him toward their father.

"But you can't hold me, Mom," she whispered. "I'm too heavy for you. It'll break your arms."

"Catty, come here and swing yourself over the edge," Mrs. Reed said firmly. "Now. Hang onto the gutter, and I'll hold your wrists until your father gets a grip on you. Come *on*, Catty."

As she dangled over the side, Catty heard something thud to the ground and knew it was Ginger's Keeping Box. She had a moment, even now, to feel an uprush of fury.

"Virginia Me-First," she said in her mind. And then, "Oh, why didn't I take mine?" It all came of not waking up fast. It all came of —

She was in her father's arms and out of them, running after Lexy, as bidden. A moment later Ginger, too, was down, and then Mrs. Reed scrambled off the side of the porch, fell into her husband's arms and, although she was a small woman, knocked him to the ground.

Lexy started forward, but Catty grabbed his arm. "Stop, Lex. They're okay. See, they're getting up."

A police car, its red roof light revolving, sending bloody flashes into the night, stood at the curb. Sirens shrieked louder and louder as two fire engines drew up and seemed scarcely to stop before orange-coated firemen were streaming over the lawn with hoses and hatchets, shouting directions, yelling for people to stand back.

"Over there — no, farther, farther back! Give us room!"

The Reeds, in all the noise and heat, were the only quiet ones, watching as flames shot in and out of the ground floor windows, crawled like bright caterpillars up the walls, as sparks flew into the darkness with a holiday air, and heat pulsed toward the spectators, who drew back, eyes fixed and fascinated.

"It's horrible," Ginger said. "Horrible. All our things."

"Not all yours," Catty muttered.

Lexy, frankly enthralled, stared open-mouthed. "Catty," he whispered, so that she had to lean over to hear him. "Catty is our whole house going to be burned up? Burned down, I mean?"

Catty took a moment to wonder if a house burned up or down or both, then told Lexy she didn't know what was going to happen, and anyway it wasn't their house any more. They'd sold it to some people named O'Hara, who were supposed to move in on the weekend. Catty wondered what would happen now. Maybe they'd have to take the house back and live in the ruins, like war victims.

"When I think of the way Mom made us clean that

42

place," Virginia said, sounding extremely put out. "And now look."

But everything we *own*, just about, Catty thought, all boxed and crated, in there ready for the moving men. Ready, now, for the fire. It was like packing up your belongings for the burglars, making it easy for them. All they had left, besides Virginia's Keeping Box, was what their father had stored in the station wagon that afternoon, and now the firemen wouldn't let Daddy drive it out of the garage.

Mr. Reed was arguing with the fire chief. "Look, Chief," he said desperately. "All we've got in the world is what's in that car. It isn't as if it were an attached garage. Look — the fire's nowhere near it yet. Just let me get the wagon out and — "

"Nope." The chief's eyes were on his men. "No way. Thing could go up in a second. We're wetting down the garage good. Chances are the wagon'll be fine."

"Chances are," Mr. Reed said bitterly.

"Look, Mister — you're lucky, darned lucky, you and your family. I've known people burn in their beds, from fires at night this way. Known whole families die of smoke poisoning — "

"Okay, okay. Spare the kids the details, will you?"

"Not that I don't feel for you. Know how you feel, exactly. *Fires!*" he said, his eyes hardening. "But you're lucky," he repeated. "Any idea how this happened?"

"No," said Mr. Reed in an exhausted voice. "I can't understand it. I have no idea at all."

He was holding his wife's hand. His other hand rested on Lexy's head. "Of course we're lucky."

Catty, standing a little apart, hating the odor and the uproar and the enormous-seeming crowd of people nearly all in their nightclothes, shivered in the heat. Except for the firemen in their uniforms, she and her family were just about the only people dressed. She thought of the expression, "All he had was what he stood up in," and wondered if this was perhaps all they were going to have to go to Vermont in. Or even if they would have a station wagon to go there in.

And my books, she moaned. My books. And all I had left of Beau, all in the Keeping Box she'd left behind because she'd been too sleepy to think. Despair and shame shook her. And which would she have tried to save, if she'd thought to save either? The books, the Box, both so important.

"You may keep one or the other," said that voice out of the Brothers Grimm, the stern voice which constantly set impossible tasks and choices before the youngest child. "Lie to your father or be a goose girl." "Very well, I'll be a goose girl." Or, "Very well, I'll give up the books." Oh, agony. "I'll give up the books, so I can have my Keeping Box."

But she had neither.

She wanted very much to cry, but judged it wasn't time yet, so concentrated on praying that the books and the Keeping Box would both come safely through the — "The Holocaust," she whispered. "The Conflagration."

Chapter 6

It was Beau himself who'd made them, the Keeping Boxes, smoothly polished chests of walnut wood with brass fittings. Catty remembered that once when somebody had asked Beau what he "wanted to be," that question people feel obliged to ask of anyone between the ages of five and twenty, he had been carefully fitting the hinges on one of the boxes.

He'd looked at his questioner helplessly, and finally lifted his shoulders. "How can I tell? The choices are so dazzling."

Beau had loved to do so many things that Mr. Reed said it was a pity he didn't have the resources to be a dilettante. In reply to Catty's question, her father said, "A dilettante is one with a refined and cultivated taste and talent for a great many arts and pursuits. The diffi-

45

culty is that nobody ever heard of a poor dilettante."

"How about Thoreau?" Beau had asked and his father had looked at him with considerable pleasure.

Beau had been a wild appearing boy, long and thin and strong as a piece of rope, with uproarious black hair and greenish eyes beneath dark heavy brows that surged together when he was thinking. To Catty, he looked like Percy Bysshe Shelley with muscles.

Beau loved sports and camping and canoeing and swimming and the woods. He loved carpentry and carving figures in wood. He loved listening to music. "Bach or rock," he'd say. "Just put something on and let's listen." He loved girls and dancing and books and talking and lying around in a hammock, in the summer, saying nothing; or tramping through the snow for miles in the winter, looking for winter birds.

He loved animals.

But that, Catty used to tell herself, was not the right way to put it. When she'd read *Wuthering Heights,* where Nellie asked Catherine whether she loved Heathcliff and Catherine said no, she didn't love Heathcliff anymore than she loved herself, Catty had thought of Beau. "I *am* Heathcliff!" Catherine had cried. Well, Beau didn't love animals, he *was* animals. He exulted in being alive and wanted to do all the things a man alive could do, but Catty was sure that Beau would have offered his life to save from extinction one species of animal. And it wouldn't have mattered what species, either — the beautiful hunted cheetah or some homely marsupial that spent most of its time asleep anyway. Beau would have died for them.

46

A fanatic, actually, her brother Beau had been.

"Living with Beau," Mrs. Reed had said once, "is like living in a country subject to earthquakes. The landscape can be calm and studded with flowers, the sky blue above you, probably a picnic going on with hotdogs and softball, and all of a sudden the ground opens and there you are, at the bottom of a crevass."

Moody was a word other people used. Temperamental, unpredictable. But alive, alive, alive . . .

After the funeral, with that flag over the coffin and the rain falling and people from all over town coming, even people who hadn't known him, because they'd read in the newspaper that Beaufort Reed had been a hero and people liked to see heroes buried, the Reeds had gone back to their house and sat around the living room wondering what to do next.

She might have been spared for years, but Catty learned at twelve that when you are in pain, when you know that what you are feeling now is sorrow, grief, those words in a book, you are quite alone even if people you love are all around you, feeling what you are feeling. You are in a sealed-off place being beaten raw but not quite to unconsciousness and there is no point in crying out because no one can hear you.

They had sat in the darkening living room, Ginger crying steadily and monotonously on the sofa; Lexy looking pinched and pale and the only one uncertain, in a way, because he was so young, of why things were the way they were; and their parents, for the first time in their lives not offering any word of help or advice to get them past a hard spot.

47

Suddenly Catty had said, "In a country where there are earthquakes, you always know that something's going on."

Her mother had looked at her quickly, with concern. She doesn't remember saying that about him, Catty thought. She thinks I'm delirious or something.

It served, anyway, to get them moving. Mrs. Reed lit a couple of lamps and said she'd fix something to eat, and to their surprise, they ate some of it.

But I was right, Catty thought months later. Since Beau, we're like a country where nothing's going on underneath or overhead or in the next valley. Could it really have been just Beau who'd kept them all tingling with the sense that anything — anything at all in the world — could happen to them, this family in a so-so house in a suburb of Indianapolis? Beau, who had spent a good part of his childhood in the Emergency Room of the local hospital and not so much because he was reckless as because he was curious about things he wasn't old enough to be curious about. A broken leg when he was five because he'd climbed too high in quest of an empty bird's nest. A broken arm and nose when he was eight because he couldn't reach the brake once he'd got the car started. Rabies shots at ten because he'd tried to comfort a dog that seemed "upset," and the dog had bitten him and run off never to be seen again. Countless stitches and bruises and scars and scares.

And, as he grew older, the always increasing closeness to that other world — the one of animals and fish and plants and birds — the world that couldn't speak and was dying because of the need and greed of the world that could.

"You see, Dad," he'd say, leaning forward and talking urgently, as he always did, as if he might forget something if he didn't hurry, "People have to be made to understand the danger that Nature is in. Do you realize that we've rendered extinct fifty species of animals in this century? Do you know that in twenty-five years there probably won't be a whale or a dolphin left in the ocean, or a big cat in the bush? That we've fouled just about every river and stream and brook and lake in this country, maybe in the world? That some of them are as dead as if they'd been murdered, like by gangsters? Do you know asphalt highways and housing developments and shopping centers are going to swallow up what little wilderness we have left if somebody doesn't fight to preserve it?"

"Of course I realize all that," Mr. Reed said. "What interests me — alarms me, is perhaps the word — is that your fervor for salvation never seems to embrace human beings."

"*Human beings.* It's human beings got us into all this mess. I think it would've been better if mankind had stayed a fish. Then maybe the other fishes and the animals and trees would've stood a chance."

"For a boy who reads Darwin so much, you've got some pretty rudimentary scientific notions. And you'll forgive me if I continue to believe that men are more important than trees or animals."

"And you'll forgive me if I don't in any way agree.

49

Besides, if you want to look at the matter from a purely self-serving — that is, human — point of view, we aren't going to have any *oxygen* left, or food, if we keep on the way we're going."

"I guess," Mr. Reed said, "that some people catch Thoreau like an incurable disease."

Looking at his father's attentive, rather troubled face, Beau had said earnestly, "It's not just Thoreau and *then*. It's us and now and the future. That's what I'm talking about. Don't you see?"

In matters like this, Catty couldn't tell what her own real feelings were because she had to side with Beau. As necessary, and as lacking in self-mastery as the coursing of her blood, was her need to be on Beau's side in everything, always.

Even now, when the winter had passed and the spring had passed, and Beau had been gone so long that he sometimes seemed like someone glorious and dear she had read of in a book, she believed everything he had believed.

When she came to realize that the constant, fusing pain she had felt for months had lessened some time when she wasn't noticing, so that she would go a few hours without missing Beau, or miss him without wanting to crawl away somewhere and cover her head, when she realized that something in her was trying to be happy, wanted to be happy, then she cried at this new loss. Maybe, she thought, reaching out her hand as though to grasp at something, maybe we will forget him. Or remember him fondly, rationally. The idea seemed to fold over her, stifling, sadder than anything else she'd thought or dreamed of.

Things happened to them, to their family, that Beau now was no part of, would never know about. He did not know that Daddy had lost his job, that Ginger's braces were finally off, that they were all moving to Vermont to work in a family business. He did not know or care that their house was burning in the night before their eyes. All this was going on and Beau knew nothing of it.

Nothing, nothing, nothing . . .

"Catty," said Mr. Reed. "Catty, what's wrong? I mean — " He laughed. "I mean, what else is wrong? Why are you looking like that?"

Catty did not say, as she'd said so often in past months, "I was thinking of Beau." Either her mother and father didn't want to talk about him, or couldn't. It had taken her all this time to see that her own need to talk maybe hurt them terribly, and that Virginia had probably been right.

She said, "I'm just hoping my box, my Keeping Box, will be all right. I hope it doesn't get burned, that's all."

Virgina said, "You can put your mind at rest about that, anyway. This one's yours." She pointed to the box on the ground.

"You mean you saved the wrong one?" Catty gasped.

"I mean I saved the one with Beau's things in it. I didn't have anything but one snapshot of him in mine. I saved the most important one."

Catty lived to be a very old woman. She outlived her

parents, her sister, her little brother, her husband Duncan, and some of her own children. And when she was very old, turning over memories like cards as old people do, one of those she came across most often was not that bearing the wild poetic picture of Beau, or of her husband, whom she'd loved, or of the son they had had who looked like Beau and was named for him. The card that seemed to come up most often now in her great age was one that bore the likeness of her sister, Virginia, red hair tangled, face flickering rosily in the light of the dying fire, smiling her gorgeous new smile as she said, "I saved the most important one."

"I loved you that night," the old woman would whisper to the sister of long ago. "I wish I had told you that once I really loved you."

Because in their lives that was the closest moment that Catherine and Virginia Reed ever had. They were too unlike to develop a friendship, too uneasy with each other to speak of things that mattered, so the moment passed.

Chapter 7

In less than an hour the firemen had turned the horrible beauty of the blaze into a smoldering stinking mess. It was not, the fire chief said, by any means the worst he had seen. Part of the house still stood, a good part of the second floor was salvageable. The basement playroom, where the fire had apparently started in a short circuit, was a loss, and much of the clapboard siding. The first floor was pretty well shot and of course the whole house would need —

He seemed to find something in Mr. Reed's face that cut short this catalog of good fortune. "You're covered, insurance-wise?" he asked solicitously.

"Probably. If anybody's ever really covered by an insurance policy, which I doubt. It's a bit more complicated than that. We just sold the place." He sighed heavily. "We'll face it all in the morning, I guess."

"Sure, sure, everything'll look better in the morning."

Mr. and Mrs. Heller, their neighbors of years, took them in for what remained of the night, fixing coffee for their parents, milk and cookies for the children. Lexy went to bed in the guest room and fell asleep right away. Mr. and Mrs. Reed stayed up in the living room and after a while the Hellers tactfully retired and left them to their problem. Catty and Ginger were put in the bedroom of a daughter away at school.

"What happens now, Ginny?" Catty asked, sitting on the bed in a borrowed nightie, arms clasped around her knees.

Ginger, in the other bed, lay with her hands under her head, staring upward. "I'm not sure," she said in a forlorn voice. "The way those firemen were slamming around with their hatchets and flooding the neighborhood with their hoses, I bet there isn't anything left in the house worth taking. And what does Daddy tell the O'Haras?"

"O'Haras?"

"Oh, Cat. The people who bought the house. Sometimes I wonder if you're altogether bright." There was no vigor in the statement, and Catty didn't take offense. So, she'd forgotten for a moment who the O'Haras were.

She looked at the Keeping Box on the floor beside her. "Ginny, did I say thank you? For my Box?"

"I guess you did. You don't have to. You aren't the only one who loved Beau."

"I didn't say — "

"Catty, I don't want to talk."

"What do you want to do?"

"Pull the blanket over my head and scream."

It seemed to Catty as good a thing to do as any. Trying to think just put her own head in a scramble. The car had been saved, so that much stuff was okay — the things in their suitcases that Daddy had packed in the station wagon this afternoon. Yesterday afternoon, it was, now. But what happened about their scorched and soaked furniture, and all those barrels with dishes and things? Since the fire chief had said a good part of the second floor was all right, did that mean her books were?

And what, now that Ginger had brought it up, did they do about the O'Haras? When people bought a house they didn't expect to find it mostly burnt when they moved in.

"Ginger?"

"Yes."

"It seems like Fate, doesn't it? I mean, that Aunt Marian should have to leave Vermont just as we have to leave Indiana. I mean, if we'd stayed here, maybe we'd have had to go on relief, like those other people Daddy told us about."

Aunt Marian, it seemed, had lived and worked with Great-uncle Henry for so many years that she didn't feel she could just walk out and leave him. "But this," she wrote to her sister, "was my chance for happiness. And what am I to do?" she appealed in that letter. "I can't let George—" or maybe it was John, "—I can't let John go, and his home and work are in California. But I can't, either, leave Uncle Henry. That is, I suppose we could get an assistant for him, but it wouldn't be the same and I'm not even sure he'd have it. It's always been such a family affair, this inn. It isn't as if it were a hotel requiring managers and bookkeepers and a corps of bellhops. When you come down to it, Unk and I, with a boy from the college to help part-time, *are* the staff. Honestly, Amy, I don't know what to do. Perhaps we should sell the place? Do you and Jim have any ideas?"

Catty had not heard the whole letter that night, as she'd fallen asleep, but the next day her mother gave it to her, and that was what it had said, only a lot more.

So now there was a resolution for the predicament. The Reeds were the resolution. They were going to move to Vermont and become innkeepers and Aunt Marian could go with a clear conscience with John to California.

"I never in my whole life," Virginia said suddenly, "*heard* of anyone stopping being a chemical engineer who'd started being one. It doesn't make sense."

"I expect there are lots of things you haven't heard of that have happened anyway. Mom says no man should work at just one job all his life. She says changes are good for people, and Daddy's lucky to have this chance."

"She has to say something bracing." Ginger yawned. "Who knows, maybe it will be good for us. Maybe horrible, of course. If we could see into the future, I wonder what we'd do, shake Fortune's hand, or run screaming for the hills? I'm just glad I got my teeth straightened before all this happened, that's all I have to say."

"My sister, the megalomaniac," Catty muttered to herself, lying awake in the Hellers' daughter's bedroom, wondering what would happen tomorrow. Today, that was.

Today they were supposed to start for Vermont, and she wondered, as at length she steered toward sleep, whether they'd just get in the station wagon and take off, leaving the O'Haras to find the new house smoking and smelling and filled with the water-logged junk of years.

"Surprise, surprise," she murmured dreamily to the O'Haras. "It's a housewarming."

Chapter 8

When he was fifteen, Beau had come home with a big button on his sweater, saying, "Don't trust anyone over 30." He'd worn it for days until Mr. Reed said, "I hope you don't really feel that way, Beau, but may I point out that whether you do or you don't trust anyone over thirty, it's rude to your mother and me to wear that sign announcing it. We do our best to be worthy of your trust."

"I don't mean you and Mom."

"Well, thanks. But we're over thirty, and we're the ones faced with that button several hours of the day, and it's beginning to undermine our self-confidence."

"Well, gee, Dad. I'm sorry you take it like that."

"I can't think how else we're supposed to take it. The

message isn't subtle. Well, put it another way, how do you take it? What does that — that slogan mean to you?"

"It means that people your age have pretty well loused up the world. Not you and Mom directly or intentionally, undertsand, but you're part of the structure that — "

Mr. Reed had flapped his hand irritably. "The human race has been steadily lousing up the world since the world, or, that is, the human race, began. I'll go along with you on that. But I won't take more than my due share of the blame, and neither will you when the time comes. And remember, youth is a self-limiting condition. That's something you kids seem unaware of, all of you."

Beau had removed the button, but he hadn't thrown it away. Mrs. Reed had found it in his drawer when she'd tried to clean up his room after the funeral. It had been Mrs. Heller finally who actually did straighten up most of Beau's modest affairs. She'd given away his clothes and nearly all his possessions, at Mrs. Reed's request.

The bronze star had come long after Beau was gone. It arrived with a specially printed sort of diploma in a dark red binder, saying how Beaufort Reed, at complete disregard for his own life and safety, had, under heavy enemy attack, crawled one hundred yards across a fire-raked meadow to drag back to the bunker an eighteen-year-old Marine who'd been lying unable to move because of leg wounds. The bronze star, attached to a striped ribbon, shone dully in its flat box.

The day it came Mrs. Reed cried until she got sick. She'd wanted to mail star and citation back to the government, and when Mr. Reed got home that evening she had it all wrapped and addressed to The President, The White House, Washington, D.C.

"Let him have the thing," she'd said in a bitter trembling voice. "He, and all these *leaders* we have, sent Beau over there, so let them have the medals for action. It's the nearest to action any of them ever get. Old men seeing to it that boys are killed — that's their kind of action, and they should have the medals for it."

Mr. Reed had put his arms around his wife and held her for a long time as she cried more and more, the two of them on the sofa, and the three children moving nervously from room to room, until at length Mrs. Reed agreed to go to bed, to go to sleep.

The next day she unwrapped the package and said only that perhaps Beau would have wanted them to keep it. "And since I'll never know what he would have wanted — " She turned away.

Lexy kept the medal for a while, and then it was put in Catty's Keeping Box, where the nicest pictures of Beau and most of his letters were. Mrs. Reed had nothing, not even a photograph of him, and for a long time she wouldn't say his name.

Catty had also taken the button saying *Don't Trust Anyone Over 30,* but its message was, for her, meaningless. There were people over thirty on whom she relied implicitly, and she knew some under twelve she wouldn't trust with a dollar or a private thought.

Just the same, she told herself during the days while they stayed with the Hellers, there were advantages to being still practically—in the world's eye—a child. One of them was that you didn't have to worry about what to tell the O'Haras when they saw their new house with a good part of it charred like a log in an outdoor fireplace. You didn't have to worry about seeing the insurance men. When the man who said he was the insurance adjustor had arrived at the Hellers', Catty had taken one look and fled upstairs to Virginia.

"He looks horrible, Ginny. He's got this teeny weeny straight mouth."

"Daddy will handle him."

"Maybe. He's a terribly cross-looking man, even before he starts talking. Perhaps," she went on, more interested than worried, "we're really going to be paupers. Did you ever read *The Prince and the Pauper*?"

"Some of it."

"Did you like it?"

"No."

"Neither did I."

"Is there some point to this conversation?"

"I don't know. I was just saying that we might be paupers and that made me think of — "

"Lovely thought to launch us on our new life with."

It appeared, though, after a few days, that Mr. Reed had contrived to calm the O'Haras and convince the insurance adjustor that he had not personally set fire to the house, and at length they got in the station wagon one morning, waved good-bye to the Hellers, and started for Vermont.

Catty, twisting around on her seat to stare over the suitcases for a last look at their house, felt a pain like cracking that ran all through her and had nothing to do with the position of her body. Their house, the one house she'd known, the house Beau had grown up in and gone away from and never come back to. Their *home*. Once they turned the corner they'd never see it again.

I don't think I can stand this, Catty thought. I really truly don't — I *cannot*. She fought to keep control of herself, because there was, in this car, a sense of pain and loss like flood waters threatening a dam. Her mother and father sat rigidly looking ahead. Ginger, by a window, had her face turned away so that all Catty could see was the long mantle of hair. Even Lexy, usually primed with joy at the thought of an adventure, sat staring at his shoes, his mouth turned down. Catty felt that if one of them said a word, shed a tear, made a sound at all, the dam would go, misery would flood over them, and Daddy would just pull over to the side of the road and they'd wait, and never move again. They'd let the pain lap over them and they'd drown.

But they turned a corner and drove down the main street and up the ramp onto the turnpike into the fast traffic, where Mr. Reed, who'd been driving slowly, was forced to pick up speed, and that was as if a release button had been pushed and they were all free to move and speak again.

"Well," said Mr. Reed, on a gusty sigh, "we're off."

Mrs. Reed put her hand on his shoulder, turned to look at the three children. "You know, I've been thinking. In a way, in a funny way, I grant you, but still — it's as if losing practically all our possessions has set us free for a totally new life."

"An omen," said Catty, whose books had come through the fire smelling of scorch but otherwise safe. "A good omen."

There was another silence, and then a discussion began about how early in the day they should break their trip. Lexy was for finding a motel with a swimming pool and stopping there at noon. Mr. Reed tentatively suggested that he just drive right on through, as they had all known he would.

"With your mother and me taking turns driving, we could make Vermont in about eighteen hours. Couldn't you kids sleep back there?"

"You mean sitting straight up like this?" Virginia demanded. "If we move an inch in any direction we run into a suitcase, you know."

"Well, I guess it isn't such a good idea," Mr. Reed conceded. On a trip he disliked even stopping for gas, which was one reason why the Reeds never took automobile vacations in the way of other families. The Hellers, last summer, had driven west, stopping at national parks all the way, but Catty and Ginger figured that if their father ever took them on such a trip they'd probably drive straight to California and back without ever getting out of the car.

"Are we really going to stay overnight in a motel?" Lexy asked, beginning to be overwhelmed by the idea even though he'd presented it first.

"Of course," said their mother. "And it's going to be fun. We'll find a nice place and stop early, as Lexy suggests, and — well, it'll be fun."

We'll make it be, Catty thought. We're a family on

our way to a new life and we're having a good time. We'll pretend that Beau is someplace else, which he is, and we'll take pleasure in what we're doing.

"Sure it's going to be fun," Mr. Reed said heartily. "We are going to have a great time, and I guarantee you'll all love Vermont. It's a beautiful state, not yet totally loused up by people as — " He cleared his throat, " — as Beau used to say,"

Then, for a long while, there was silence again and the miles rolled away behind them as they moved farther and farther away from their house, from their life as it had been, as they left Beau farther and farther behind them.

Chapter 9

"This looks like a nice place," Mrs. Reed said, quite as if it were not the fourth or fifth time she'd straightened as they approached a motel and observed that it looked like a nice place, only to have Mr. Reed respond, "Too bad. We've already passed it," as he drove by.

He'd done the same whenever one of the children spied a Dairy Queen ahead, or a service area with a restaurant. He'd slow down slightly, look in his rear view mirror and pick up speed, saying, "Couldn't stop. That fellow was right on my tailboard."

"Mother!" Virginia wailed at last. "We want to stop! I think my muscles are atrophied from sitting in one position for so long."

"What's atrophied?" said Lexy.

"Frozen stiff."

"No," said Mr. Reed. "It means wasted. From lack of nourishment, usually." He seemed to realize his mistake the moment the words were out, because his entire family, including his wife, assured him that in that case they were atrophied.

"Okay," he said with a sigh. "We're just about out of gas anyway. Next place we see, we'll stop."

The next place was The Mountain View Motel. Mrs. Reed, looking at the service stations to either side, the shopping center across the wide turnpike, and the flat landscape reaching in all directions, said, "Wonder where the mountain is that we're supposed to view."

"Leveled to make room for the motel, perhaps," said her husband.

As they drove into the courtyard and pulled up before the office, Catty felt her stomach sink. A tide of home-sickness washed over her. I want to be *home,* she moaned inwardly. I want my own room and my own — my own —

I don't want to be here or go to Vermont or live with Uncle Henry. I want to go back, to go back —

"Look," Mrs. Reed said. "There's a lovely swimming pool. Look at the fountain in it. And there are lots of children your age. It should be great fun."

"Whose age?" Ginger asked irritably, and Catty suspected that she, too, was nervous of the unknown.

"I don't want to swim," Lexy said loudly. "I won't go in that pool with a whole lot of kids I don't know."

"Oh, for Pete's sake," said Mr. Reed. "I thought you wanted a motel with a swimming pool and a playground, and now I find you a place that looks more like a resort than an overnight stop and you're all whining."

"Who's whining?" Ginger asked. "I haven't been whining. Neither," she added unexpectedly, "has Catty."

"You don't have to *say* things to communicate a whine. I can tell by looking around me that nobody's having any fun — "

"Darling," said Mrs. Reed. "Why don't you go in and register and get us rooms. One for the girls, and Lexy can be with us, all right?"

"Sure, sure. Fine." He got out and walked into the room marked Office, not looking back, as he usually did when he walked away from people.

"What's the matter with him?" Ginger demanded.

Mrs. Reed turned around in her seat and fixed them, one after the other, with a stern eye. "Now, you three listen, and listen carefully. Your father is under a terrible strain, and I re*quire* that even if you don't understand how a man who has lost a job through no fault of his own and then lost a good deal of what he'd saved because of a fire — "

"You mean our savings are gone, too?" Ginny said sharply.

"You hush, Virginia. I mean it. Ordinarily your father and I take you into our confidence about nearly everything because that's how we think a family should be, but at this particular time your father has quite enough to face and worry about without having his children moping and sniveling." She lifted her hand as Ginny seemed about to protest. "Moping and sniveling. We

67

can't discuss all of this with you because we aren't sure ourselves what we're doing, but I'd hope you'd have enough faith in us just to go along with things for a while — "

"Sure we do, Mom," Catty said. "It's just — well, it's scary, all this new stuff happening all together."

"I know it is," said Mrs. Reed. She did not add, but Catty could feel her unsaid, "Your father and I are scared, too," and it made her shiver.

Mr. Reed came out, got in, looked at some keys he was carrying. "Rooms 462 and 463, adjoining bath. Let's go."

Mrs. Reed had packed two small suitcases with night-clothes and a change of underwear, suitcases that could be easily got at, and when they were in front of their rooms, she said, "That's for you two, Ginger. This is for us. I put bathing suits in."

Room 462 seemed, to the two girls, enormous, vastly neat and bland. Vanilla-colored furniture, two double beds, a television set bolted to a stand, violently flowered draperies and candlewick bedspreads, sleazily thin, the color of dried mud.

"Yuck," said Virginia, looking around.

Catty opened the bathroom door, knocked on the opposite door and said to Lexy, who opened it, "Let's see your room."

It was the same, just occupying another space. Not one single thing different from the room she and Ginny were in.

"It's nice, isn't it, Mom?" Catty said carefully, and her father burst into laughter.

"You are a good dear sweet obliging character," said

Mr. Reed. "And I want to say, on behalf of the firm and the stockholders and the Board of Directors, that your efforts are appreciated. Some tangible token will doubtless be forthcoming."

Catty grinned at him. "No, but it's okay, Daddy. Come on, Lex. Let's put on our bathing suits and go to that pool."

Lexy hesitated. "You gonna come, Dad?"

"Well — "

"Lexy, for Pete's sake, can't you and I go? Maybe Ginny will come with us."

But Ginny would not. "Leave me alone, Catty," she said. "I just want to be *alone* for a while."

"Okay, your royal highness," said Catty, pulling on her bathing suit. "Your wish is my command." She got a towel from the bathroom, came back to say, "But Mom is right. You're a rotten sport."

"Go away," Ginger said scratchily. "Just go away."

Lexy and Catty walked at a nervous pace across a grass area toward the pool, which seemed, to their timid vision, to be swarming with people. Swarming with strangers. Catty's mouth was dry and she could feel Lexy trembling beside her.

He tugged roughly at her hand. "Let's go back, Cat. Everybody's looking at us."

Catty swallowed noisily. "Everybody is *not* looking at us," she said in a hoarse voice. She cleared her throat. "That's just dumb, Lex. Why should they look at us?"

"Because they got here first," said Lexy, going to the point as usual.

"We've got as much right here as anybody else."

"Yeah, but I want to go *back*. I don't like places where everybody got here first."

She looked down at his skinny body with its big hands and feet, its knobby knees. She looked into the huge gray eyes and refused their appeal.

"What's the matter with you, Lex? You usually like to do new things. You're the adventurous one in the family now that — you're the one who likes to encounter the unknown."

"I like to encounter the unknown at home where I know what it is," he said. Catty giggled, and in a moment Lexy gave a faint answering smile.

"The trouble with us," she said to him, "is we're hicks, Lexy."

"Hicks, how?" he croaked.

"We've never been *any*place, do you realize that?"

"I wish I wasn't anyplace now. I wish we was all home."

"Wish we *were* home."

"That's what I said."

"No, but I'm trying to explain why we're nervous. People who have never been anyplace strange in their lives before are scared of strange places, that's all."

"It's enough. Catty, let's go back."

"No," she said firmly, taking his hand. "We're doing this for Daddy. And Mom. We're going to make them think we're having fun. Lex, you could pretend you're having fun, couldn't you? You're good at pretending."

"I'm good at pretending things I want to pretend. I don't want to pretend in there with all those people, Cat."

They were at the fence now, that surrounded the pool. Catty glanced back, saw her mother at the window. She waved, and Catty waved gaily back.

"Wave, Lex," she ordered. "Wave to Mom. She's watching."

"Oh, gee whiz," Lexy mumbled, flapping his hand toward the motel rooms. "I want to go back home, Catty. I *hate* this."

Catty wiped a hand across her mouth. "We got this far. We can at least go in and splash a bit. That fountain looks like it'd be fun. Come on, Lexy," she coaxed. "I'll be with you."

Then, when they were in the pool, splashing around under the airy stream of the fountain, they forgot they were pretending and had a wonderful time.

Going back to their rooms, Catty had an idea, so thrilling to her, so full of promise, that she stopped walking and stood perfectly still in the grass.

Lexy, who'd gone on, turned and said, "What're you doing, Catty? You step on something?"

"No," she answered gently, to disturb as little as possible this awareness that was reaching her. "No. I just had a — a thought."

"About what?" He came back, looking curious.

"I can't explain."

"Oh."

"I mean, maybe I will sometime, but I can't just yet."

"Okay," he said, losing interest. "You want to stand here for a while?"

"No, no it's all right. We'll go and get dressed."

"Well, was it fun?" Ginny asked with an air of not

71

caring, after Catty had dressed and hung her bathing suit over the shower rod.

Catty nodded. "There's a fountain."

"I saw it."

Ginger had her transistor radio on and was brushing her hair at the naked vanity table, stopping now and then to examine her teeth with grave attentiveness. Catty lay down on one of the double beds and looked at the ceiling, examining, in turn, her new idea.

If you were afraid of things — no matter what or how many — what you were afraid of, really, was facing what you were afraid of. Closets, thunderstorms, parties, the dark—they were frightening because she wouldn't face them. Like Lexy, today, she'd been terrified to go over to that swimming pool because she thought it was full of strangers who might look at her, even though she knew, at the same time, that those people were also strangers to one another and would *not* look at her. And wouldn't affect anything in her life if they did look at her.

With all these conflicts shaking her badly, she still had gone so that their parents, especially Daddy, wouldn't feel everything they did was a flop. She pretended not to be afraid, so that Lexy wouldn't be, and what came out of all that was that she *hadn't* been afraid.

"Ginger?" she said tentatively.

"Yes?"

"I've decided I'm not afraid anymore."

"Not afraid of what?"

"Anything."

"That's silly. Nobody's not afraid of anything."

"Oh, no . . . I mean, of course you have to be afraid of things that you're supposed to be afraid of. That's not what I'm talking about. What I mean is — I was thinking that if you're afraid of things you needn't be afraid of, like strange places just because they're strange, it's maybe because you're thinking just about how *you* think about things yourself, you know? But if you're thinking about somebody else and how *they* feel, you forget to be afraid. Or you stop. Or something," she trailed off, because her sister had turned, hairbrush dangling in her hand, an expression of almost sarcastic tolerance on her face.

"That's dandy," said Virginia. "When we get to Vermont and you're going to a new school, I'll be very grateful if you remember this conversation, so maybe I won't have to keep on taking you to school until you're a senior in college."

Her voice shook a little, and when she turned back to brush her hair her hand, too, trembled. Catty squeezed her eyes shut but could not prevent the tears that trickled down her temples. I *am* going to remember this conversation, she told herself. I'll remember, because it is very very important — to me. Maybe she wouldn't get over being afraid all at once of everything, but it was a way to start.

She tried to imprint the words across the front of her mind. *Think about how somebody else is feeling and you won't have time to be afraid.* If Ginger hadn't been there, she'd have written the words down. But she'd remember them.

And one thing I am not going to do, she told herself,

putting an arm across her eyes and wishing Ginny didn't like rock played so horribly loud, one thing I'm never going to do again is have Ginger take me to school.

My God, she thought, feeling a hot blush creep into her face, I should be ashamed even to have to say the words. I am thirteen years old, not *three*.

"I'll go to school without you," she said softly to her sister's back. "And I don't like you."

She knew that the music would cover her terrible words, that she only partly meant, but did mean, in part.

Chapter 10

The following morning they left so early that only they and one other family, far down the court, were stirring. At this hour even the turnpike seemed to achieve a relative air of peace. The air was misty over the great shopping center; the service stations; the rows of motel units, draperies drawn close to give privacy to sleeping travelers. Automobiles of all types stretched in either direction and Catty fancied you might think them resting, too, for the day that lay ahead, filled with noise and hot dogs and complaints and road maps and hours and hours of turning wheels. The neon sign over the motel coffee shop looked pallid in the morning light, but the coffee shop itself was not open.

"I'm awfully hungry," Lexy said as he climbed in the back of the station wagon, trying to close the door quietly, as his mother had asked him to, so as not to disturb people. The door seemed to make an extraordinary amount of noise and Catty frowned at him. "I can't help it," he protested. "How can you slam something without making a noise? Daddy, I'm hungry."

"Well, so am I. We'll stop the first place we find open."

He drove past the empty swimming pool, its glossy blue water ruffling slightly in the breeze. The fountain was turned off. They went around a curving ramp, past the office, and onto the turnpike where traffic already was beginning to thicken.

"Should be a Howard Johnson's or something pretty soon."

He did stop at the first place he saw open, and when they were seated at the orange formica table with its paper place mats and had ordered their breakfast from a cheery waitress in an orange and green uniform, who served Mr. and Mrs. Reed coffee without being asked, he smiled hopefully at his family.

"Everybody sleep well?"

"Sure, Dad," said Lexy and Catty together. Ginny nodded and yawned.

"Should be there by midafternoon, making an early start like this."

"I am so longing to see Marian," said Mrs. Reed.

"Mom, when's she getting married?" Catty asked, sighing with pleasure at a great plate of pancakes that had been put before her. She poured syrup liberally, not meeting her sister's eye. Ginger was having coffee, juice, and toast.

"Soon."

"Can we go to the wedding?"

"Well, naturally we'll go. We're the family."

Ginger put her cup down carefully and looked across the table at her mother. "You're sort of overdoing this, I think. *If* you want my opinion."

"Which we don't," said Catty, as her mother inquired, "Overdoing what, Ginny?"

"This *family* bit. Do you realize how many times in the past month we've been told about the family business, the family-run inn, the fact that we'll be living and working with the *family*? We don't even know these people — Catty and Lex and I. They're strangers."

Mrs. Reed lifted her cup to lips that trembled slightly, and Catty turned furiously on her sister. "You are the worst, lousiest mean-temperedest pill that anyone ever knew!" Words had a treacherous way of deserting her in times of urgency.

Virginia, barely glancing at Catty, looked back to her mother.

Mrs. Reed put her cup down. "Don't, Catty. Please. Virginia is right, of course. She so often is." There was a cutting undertone to the remark. "I guess I've been trying to force a feeling on all of you that should come by degrees. If it comes at all, of course."

"Well," said Mr. Reed. "Now that Virginia has contrived, in her usual reasonable fashion, to cast a pall over the day, shall we finish this meal and get going?"

"Oh, damn," Virginia whispered. "Damn." She lifted her head. "I apologize. I — actually did think I was being reasonable."

"And so you were," her father said, unrelenting. "Eat up, kids."

Without effort, Virginia Reed had been a straight A student since the start of school.

"Her I.Q." Beau had once told Catty, "is larger than the sum of its parts."

"I guess that's supposed to mean something."

"It means she has more I.Q. than brains. Virginia has so much going for her that it's practically robbery. She's got looks and brains to spare, and what happens? She gets everybody in a ten-mile radius so uptight they're swarming over the walls to escape. The trouble with Ginny, if you ask me, is that she's impatient with anyone whose brain isn't as fast as hers, and she shows it. And since that includes about ninety-nine per cent of the population, including most of her teachers, it figures that she's impatient with just about everybody she comes up against. And I don't think it's so brainy to show everybody else you're smarter than they are."

"Poor Ginny."

"Hmmp," said Beau. "What about poor Sam and the way she treated him?"

Sam Hirsch had been Virginia's first serious encounter with a boy. Although boys had been milling around, as Beau sometimes said, like calves at a salt lick since she'd been twelve, Ginger had paid little attention.

Then the year she was fifteen, Beau had brought his new friend, Sam, home. Sam had been in the school only since fall, and like Beau was a senior. He was handsome and winning and likely to make most likely everything that Beau didn't in the class yearbook. He could not, like the others, be ignored.

He'd taken one look at Virginia and said, aloud, "Wow. What a swell lot of looks," and fell for her like a stone dropped off a bridge.

Virginia appeared to respond. She responded, anyway, to the condition of being adored by this highly attractive boy. Sam was at their house so often that Mr. Reed had said once he felt as if they were being infiltrated. Morning, noon and night. Weekdays, weekends, holidays. Whenever Sam was free, there he was, in their midst, doting on Virginia.

One rainy evening, waiting in the living room for Virginia to appear, Sam had picked up the Sunday *New York Times,* which arrived at their house on Tuesday, and idly begun the crossword puzzle.

Ginger considered that page her own. She could do the crossword in under an hour and usually was able to finish the Double-Crostic. No one contested her for them. Because, said Mr. Reed, the rest of them would take hours for the puzzle and couldn't do the Double-Crostic at all without a dictionary, an atlas, and a research assistant. "And that," he said, "represents entirely too much time spent not doing far more interesting things, like talking or looking at football games."

Waiting for the girl he'd decided he couldn't live without, Sam had worked at the puzzle for a while and then put it to one side.

When Virginia came down, she noticed almost immediately that someone had been at her page. "Who did that?" she asked sharply.

"Huh?" said Sam, following her glance. "Oh. The puzzle. I did. I mean, I started to. You look great with that braid. Like a redheaded Indian princess."

Virginia looked around at the rest of her family, variously disposed in the living room. Mr. Reed was turning through the news section, Catty the book review, Mrs. Reed the drama section. Beau and Lexy were playing Scrabble.

"Why didn't someone tell Sam not to do that?"

"Do what?" Sam asked. "You tell me."

"All right, I will. That's *my* crossword puzzle."

"Yours?"

"Mine," she said with asperity. "*I* do the Sunday puzzle every week and everybody knows it."

"Well, Gin. Not everybody. I mean, *I* don't. Didn't. I bet not one of the linebackers of the Texas Oilers knows it, or a single member of the faculty at the University of Hawaii, or — " He went on enumerating individuals and groups who might be unaware of the fact that the Sunday *Times* puzzle page was Virginia Reed's exclusive property.

"With a sense of humor like that," Ginny said, "no door will be closed to you."

"Say, hey — " Sam said, beginning to realize she was in earnest.

"At least you could have asked. There's such a thing as manners."

"Yeah, there is, isn't there?"

With all attention now on them, Mrs. Reed attempted to quell the rising rancor. "Virginia," she said to Sam, laughing slightly, "is as possessive as a Peke with a bone about that silly puzzle page."

"I'd never have touched it if I'd known the circumstances," he said.

Virginia, oblivious to everything but her own outrage, picked up the puzzle and scanned it. "You've already made four mistakes. Amino acid is not spelled with an e, and that e makes 14 down silly. In this country we spell inquire with an i, not an e, and *that* makes — "

"A mistake. I get it." Sam stood up. "Hey, Beau, I find I gotta run. See you tomorrow. Bye, Mr. and Mrs. Reed. Catty, Lex. So long, Ginger."

In the silence that followed his departure, Virginia picked up the paper, let it fall, looked around at her family, who avoided her eye.

"Honestly," she said in a nervous voice, "the things that boy doesn't know. Look here — he thinks Yeats wrote the 'Sonnet on Sleep.' It's funny how re*veal*ing a crossword puzzle can be of a person's mind."

"Guess you're right," said Beau. "Very acute of you."

"Well — but for heaven's sake. Did he have to stamp off that way? I mean, what a lot of fuss over a puzzle. To say nothing of his *manners* — "

"The less said about manners just now, the better."

Virginia's lower lip trembled. "I don't care!" she shouted and left the room, running upstairs and slamming her door.

Mrs. Reed said sadly, "What is wrong with Ginger? Why does she act this way? She'll end up without a friend in the world."

"She doesn't have too many as it is," Catty said, feeling shaken. She found Virginia almost scary in her inability to know what other people were feeling. She could pass a chemistry test higher than anyone else in the school, but the chemistry of people was out of her scope, and it made a person — anyway, a person related to her — feel awful.

You have to care what happens to people in your family, Catty had thought that day. Whether you want to or not. If Virginia had been someone else, somebody else's sister, she'd only be a person to avoid. But your own *sister* — you had to mind about her.

Mrs. Reed seemed so troubled and nervous that her husband got up to pat her hand and say he'd make some coffee. "Don't worry, dear. She's young. She'll grow out of this — this self-interest. It's my belief that at a certain age young people have to be almost totally self-involved, self-serving, self-important. It's how they find what this *self* is, don't you think?"

"I just hope you're right," Mrs. Reed said miserably.

Catty didn't think her father was right. Or, if he was, Virginia carried his theory to sappy extremes. Thinking it over, she supposed that most of the kids she knew, herself included, were pretty absorbed in themselves, their looks, their relationships, their needs, their joys and sorrows, and so forth. But at least the rest of them seemed to recognize that other people did, after all, share the planet.

Sam had never come back to their house. Remaining Beau's friend, he shot out of the family's orbit as suddenly as he'd arrowed into it.

Ginger, unbelieving at first, then baffled, finally hurt, decided that after all she cared for him, and set out to woo him back. Waiting in school corridors, at the high school gathering places in town, she presented herself in her prettiest plumage, aired her proudest mannerisms, unable to believe that what had worked so well once — her beauty and volatile spirits — would not work again.

After a few weeks, filled with the special pain of hurt pride, she embarked on a series of flirtations, lining up the boys and shooting them down, always with an eye on Sam to see what effect it was having on him.

It had, so far as anyone ever knew, none.

The summer after they graduated, Sam and Beau took a canoe trip in Canada, and Sam did not come back. In the investigation that followed the accident it was found that when their boat overturned in a stretch of furious white water, Sam had hit his head on a rock and so drowned.

Beau told the investigators, Sam's family, his own family, their friends, that he had tried his best to save Sam. But all that was certain was that he had somehow saved himself.

Virginia, for a while, conducted herself as if a young and flamelike association had been snuffed out, but then went back to dating, getting A's, doing the Double-Crostic, and failing to interpret the human emotions that went on everywhere around her.

Especially she failed to receive the desperate signals that Beau, in bewilderment and pain, was flying before them. He condemned himself as a coward. The rest of his family, and Sam's family, too, attempted to dissuade him, but Ginny, by her frequent mournful references to Sam, did not.

Sometimes, in the months that followed, when Beau was in boot camp, when Beau was on the troopship carrying him to Vietnam, when Beau was fighting as a Marine and writing letters trying to explain how he felt about everything—war, death, life, friendship, courage, home—Catty knew a dark thought. She would wonder *why* you had to care about your sister, even if you didn't like or understand her at all.

Chapter 11

There was a town square with a green in the center and a bandstand in the center of the green. There was a general store with a sign, "Self Service," dangling from the original sign which read, "Groceries & Dry Goods, R. F. Bull, Prop." There was a small, brand-new Post Office, a seedy two-pump gas station with an acre of wrecked cars piled behind it. Across the green was a white clapboard church, lacy, immaculate, its slender steeple topped with a goldfish weather vane.

"I don't know much about Congregationalists," said Mr. Reed, driving slowly, "but they certainly build the most beautiful churches in the world."

Halfway around the square he stopped the car briefly and sat back to regard the church as he would a painting. To one side of it was the parish house, to the other an ancient graveyard with simple tombstones, tilted and time-smoothed. It was almost well-kept, but clearly no one had been buried there in a long time.

"How quiet it is," Catty said.

"It's a graveyard," said Lexy. "Gotta be quiet."

"I wasn't talking about the graveyard. The town is so little and quiet."

"It's getting on for supper time," said Mr. Reed. "Most people are at home now."

He started the motor and drove north, out of town along a winding two-lane road. They'd gone a little over two miles when he slowed, turned into a driveway, and stopped with an air, now, of stopping for good.

The house, built of rosy old bricks, stood not far back from the road. It was large, with a weathered gray barn beside it and a meadow sweeping up behind to disappear over a hilltop. Beyond were woods. Above the wide, dark blue door of the house was a fanlight surmounted by a wooden eagle, and at the windows were dark blue shutters. The paint was peeling on shutters and door.

At this hour the air was filled with the songs of birds, and swallows seemed to ski across the meadow and around the barn.

"Why, it's a beautiful house," Virginia said. "You never told us how beautiful it is."

"Yes," said Mrs. Reed. "I did tell you."

Virginia was looking at the house much as her father had looked at the church.

Suddenly Mrs. Reed was running from them, into the arms of a woman who'd come through the door.

"Marian!"

"Amy . . . oh, Amy! Oh, I am so glad to see you. Let me *look* at you."

They held each other at arm's length, then embraced again, while the children regarded this encounter with mild wonder. To them, Aunt Marian was a person seen once, mentioned fairly frequently, telephoned now and then, written to rarely. Now here she was, real, and bringing a note of joy to their mother's voice they hadn't heard in months.

"Children!" she caroled. "Children, come and greet your Aunt Marian."

Aunt Marian was younger than their mother. Not, Catty thought, prettier. But nice-looking. Above all, you noticed at once how happy she looked. It gave her a special, splendid air.

Catty and Ginger allowed themselves to be hugged, and Aunt Marian just offered her hand to Lexy, which was, Catty thought, quick of her. She was all at once sort of sorry that this aunt she'd never given any particular thought to was going to be out of their lives so soon.

They milled about with suitcases, finally started into the house, Catty wondering if some day, way in the future, she and Ginger would greet each other with such joy. It didn't seem likely. Maybe, she decided, if we hadn't seen each other in years, we might be glad of the reencounter.

But she looked at Virginia, going gracefully up the stairs in front of her, and thought how the whole day, just about, had passed without Ginny's saying one nice word to anybody. She'd just sat, staring sideways out of the window so that you couldn't even see her face, and ignored everybody. She wouldn't play Ghosts or Twenty Questions, she wouldn't indicate a preference for a place to stop and eat. She answered her parents if there was no way to avoid it, but overlooked her brother and sister as if they weren't in the car at all.

If the most noticeable thing about Aunt Marian was her air of animation and delight, the most noticeable about Ginger was her discontent. Ginny never looks happy, Catty thought irritably, unless there is something immediate and specific to be happy about. It'd be a pleasure to poke her in the nose.

On the second-floor landing a narrow hall went to either side and contained so many doors that Catty blinked in amazement. The stairs went on up another flight. Directly before them was a huge gold-framed mirror that reflected all of them duskily, like a brown pond. She learned later that it was called a cheval glass and was, like so much else in the house, an antique of "no especial value," as Aunt Marian put it. But Catty came to love the things of this house — the nine-foot grandfather clock in the downstairs hall, the cheval glass, the worn, figured carpets — the feeling of permanence, of continuance, that these things gave her.

"Where's Uncle Henry?" Mr. Reed asked.

"He's cooking. The reason he isn't here to greet you is that he hasn't heard you. Uncle's gotten a little deaf. He may even have his hearing aid off. He often turns it off when he's working. We'll go to the kitchen directly, as soon as you've seen your rooms and washed up if you want."

"Oh, I don't think we should put off seeing him,"

Mrs. Reed began. "He might be hurt — "

"Amy! Uncle Henry get his feelings hurt? Since when? Besides, his attitude will be that since you're all going to be together from now on, there'd be no point in altering his routine. Just now the routine calls for getting the chowder made. We serve supper at 6:30. Dinner is at one. It's better to feed old people their big meal at midday."

"Are all the people here old?" Catty asked curiously.

"All the guests are. Some of the rest of us are only in the springtime of our senescence," Aunt Marian replied with an easy laugh.

"Does Unk do the cooking?" Mr. Reed asked.

"Oh yes. I do the marketing and supervise the housework, but Uncle makes up the menus and cooks, and he is *good*. I do believe if the cooking were up to me, I'd check the sky every night to be sure the world wasn't coming to an end before I started dinner."

"That'll be nice for your John," Mrs. Reed said drily.

Aunt Marian laughed again. Clearly nothing was going to trouble her. "Well, the guests have been — I mean, are — lucky that Uncle Henry is a chef."

"How many do you have? Guests?"

"Seven. Five women, two men."

"Where are they? I haven't seen a sign of them."

"I do believe they've all tactfully retired to their rooms in order to give us time to get the family settled in. Now," she said, going down the hall and opening a door, "you and Jim have your old room, remember? Virginia can have that one at the end of the hall. Catherine — Catty — I've put you and Lexy on the third floor, if that's all right with you? The rest of the rooms on this floor are occupied by the guests."

Catty glanced at her mother, who said, "Marian, I think that perhaps Virginia — "

"No," Catty interrupted. "No, really. The third floor will be fine for me." Lexy will be up there, she thought, maybe pretty close. It'll be fine."

"Well," Aunt Marian said, "I suppose we could put Catty on this floor and Virginia upst—"

"I'm tired," Virginia said. Meaning, Catty interpreted, upstairs or downstairs makes no difference to Ginny, just so she gets away from us. In a way, she understood how her sister felt. There was so much *talking* going on.

"I'd like to be on the third floor," she said firmly and started up.

Her room was small, with two dormer windows tucked between sloping eaves. There was a single bed with a patchwork quilt on it, a little wing chair, an old desk, a bedside table. A faded hooked rug lay on the dark wide board floors, and the wallpaper, green and yellow verticle stripes of flowers, was stained under the windows. From rain, probably, Catty thought. Or snow. There'd be lots of snow in Vermont, in the winter, she thought dreamily.

"Things are rather shabby, you'll find," Aunt Marian said. "We try to keep the downstairs in some kind of repair, but the farther up you go, the mangier things get. You and Lex have come the limit. I hope you don't mind. It's just that I thought somehow you'd like this room. I always have."

"It's the prettiest room I've ever seen."

There were white curtains at the window, clean and limp and thin, pulled to the sides with drawbacks. Catty could see far up the meadow, where, as she looked, a deer appeared over the rim of the hill. It stood a moment, head up, gazing about, then gently leaned over and began to nibble the grass. As Catty watched, rapt, almost unbelieving, two fawns came into view and moved delicately beside their mother.

"Aunt Marian," Catty whispered. "Look." She pointed, and found her finger was shaking slightly.

"They come out at this hour to graze. Sometimes early in the morning, too."

"It doesn't seem *possible*," Catty breathed. "I've never seen a real animal before — I mean, a wild animal, where it belongs. Only in zoos — " Her voice trailed off, and she turned. "Lex, Lexy, where are you?"

"Right behind you," he said.

"Do you see — "

"Yeah." His eyes were shining. "They're real live deers, aren't they?"

Now, at this moment, in this room, her room, with Lexy beside her and those three beautiful creatures moving on the rim of the meadow, Catty was seized with such joy that she all but called out, "Look, Beau — at the deer in the meadow!"

A tear slid down her cheek, and Aunt Marian said with quick concern, "Why, Catty. Whatever is wrong, dear?"

Catty shook her head. "I'm happy. It makes me a little sad, to be happy."

Aunt Marian didn't ask what that might mean. She

91

gave her niece a quick hug and said, "Would you like to see your room, Lexy?"

"Does it face the same way as this one?"

"It does. There are these two little rooms up here, and a bathroom, on this side, and all the other side is attic. Storage space."

Lexy sighed and smiled. "Let's go."

Chapter 12

Since she'd known they were coming to Vermont, Catty had been forming pictures of Great Uncle Henry in her mind. Sometimes he was a frail old fellow tucked under a lap rug in an overstuffed chair — an ancient, tail-thumping dog breathing heavily on the floor beside him — gently boring hearers with tales of the olden times. Then again he'd be one of those powerful old men, narrow as a board, shaking a clenched and sinewy fist in the face of age. Like King Lear, only not dotty.

Now, in the great kitchen, faced with a short rather stout man in a chef's hat who moved briskly from sink to stove, she relinquished those men in favor of this one without hesitation. Of course this was how Uncle Henry had to look, had to be.

"Well, well, well," he said, wiping his hands on a

towel at his waist. "Isn't this just great. Jim, I can't tell you what this means to me — "

"Good of you to put it that way," Mr. Reed said wryly.

"How *are* you, Jim? How's the state of your health and being?"

"Well, you know, Unk — the years fly by, and I'm afraid to comb my hair."

Uncle Henry laughed. "There isn't much under this white hat, I assure you. But you don't have to worry for a while yet, Jim." He turned and put his arms around Mrs. Reed. "Little Amy," he said fondly. "She's as pretty as ever, eh, Marian? And this is Catherine." He bowed just perceptibly. "And Alexander. Welcome to Vermont, children. I hope you're going to be happy here. Where's Virginia?"

"Still upstairs," said Mrs. Reed.

"Of course, of course. Tired out, and no wonder. I'd certainly have come out to greet you when you arrived, but I didn't hear you. Fact is, even with the hearing aid I don't hear all that goes on and a blessing it is at times, A few of the guests, God love them, would talk the ears off a jackass, but if I sail right past they attribute it to deafness and advancing years — matters they know something of first-hand." He turned back to the stove.

Catty had never seen so large a stove. Six burners, a well, a griddle, two ovens. The refrigerator, too, was enormous, and in the center of the kitchen was a great wooden table on which Uncle Henry had been rolling biscuit dough. After peering into the well of the stove and nodding approval, he began to cut out biscuits.

"Anything I can do?" Mrs. Reed asked. Uncle Henry did not reply until she moved to where he could see her and repeated the question. Catty decided he must be good at lipreading.

"Not a bit of it. I hope you're not all famished— though of course if you are we can rustle up something extra. We have supper at night. Old people need their heavier meal in the middle of the day, you know. Can't overload their bellies at bedtime. Now, this evening we're having a fish chowder, biscuits, salad, and a nice light gingerbread with whipped cream."

"That's supper?" Mrs. Reed laughed. "It would do for dinner at our house."

"Fact? Well, you must be light eaters. Anyway, isn't this your house now? Your home?"

When Mrs. Reed didn't reply, her husband said, "You're very decent to — " He got no further.

"Blast it, Jim, shall I have to endure expressions of gratitude? You have any idea the fix I'd be in for help here without Marian? We have Duncan Charters, of course. And Phil Quincy, my handyman, he's down for the count, looks like, and not that I don't feel for him, I do, but the thought of trying to keep up around here with him laid up maybe forever — it was like to give me a heart attack myself." He paused, seemed to think back over his own words. "Don't mean to imply that you're a handyman, Jim — graduate engineer and all. Just temporarily, if you could —"

"Unk, you and I are going to have to have a talk. If I stop expressing gratitude for shelter for my family at this juncture in our lives, *and* the pleasure of your company, then you'll have to accept my help in every way you need it and I can give it. Actually, I rather plume myself on my abilities as a handyman. Ask Amy."

The sideboard, Catty saw, was stacked with pots and pans and dishes, rinsed but not washed. Probably they couldn't keep up with everything, but it was a job that someone, obviously, was going to be obliged to undertake. She glanced uneasily at her mother.

"That's a formidable sight," said Mrs. Reed. "I could start them, couldn't I?"

"Oh, no," said her sister. "Uncle and I do everything connected with the kitchen, including waiting on table, ex*cept* the dishes. We have a college boy, Duncan Charters, who comes in the evening and washes up. He has a room off the kitchen here. In the morning he does the vacuuming and dusting and makes up the guests' beds before he leaves for school. He's going to summer school to finish his four years in three. He's a lovely boy."

"Well, well, well," said Uncle Henry. "Can't remember when I've felt cheerier about things in general." He glanced at a large wooden-framed clock on the wall. "Have to get the biscuits in. Supper in twenty minutes. Let's see — I'll try to give you a rundown on the guests. We have two men, five ladies. All a bit long in the tooth, but hale. Can't keep them here when they get incapacitated. Breaks me up when I have to tell a family to take somebody and cart them off to a nursing home, but we aren't equipped here to take care of sick folks. Fact is, everybody's in good condition at this present reading. Physically, that is. Far as disposition goes, some of them aren't anyone's notion of paradise regained, but that's human nature, after all."

"What's the inn called, Uncle Henry?" Catty asked. "You don't even have a sign outside. How do people know it's an inn?"

"Well, it isn't, not in that sense. Not like a motel or hotel. We don't cater to transients. More a guesthouse, I guess you'd call it. Now, let's see, what *is* it called? Henry Wendell's place, usually. Or The Inn. Only one in town. I got these letterheads, had them for years, with *Wendell's Inn* at the top. So I guess that's it. But around here it's just called The Inn."

"Uncle Henry, we saw three deer in the meadow," Lexy said. "A mother and two babies. Fawns."

"I have salt licks scattered about the place for them. You'll see lots of creatures around here. Got a family of racoons come around to the kitchen door right after supper."

Lexy's mouth gaped open. "Honest?"

"You'll see."

Exchanging a blissful look with Lexy, Catty found herself thinking how dreadful it would have been if their father hadn't lost his job.

Later, when they'd come to know the house, it didn't seem so huge and bewildering, but on this first evening Catty thought she'd never learn her way around.

She and Lexy left their parents in the kitchen with Aunt Marian and wandered downstairs until suppertime. They went through the dining room, where a westering sun lay across tables set for supper, each with a bowl of petunias and ageratums, bright place mats, and napkins actually in napkin rings. A white chair rail ran around the room, and above it a blue-and-white medallioned wallpaper that, Catty observed, was also faintly water stained under the windows and pulling away from the walls in the corners.

Across the wide hall was a large room that by any standards had to be called a parlor. There was a bay window crowded with plants, and wide board floors, the same as upstairs, which waved a bit in places and had cracks here and there, and ancient stains. Above the mantel was an old banjo clock with a brass pendulum that swung slowly back and forth behind a small glass window. A large faded flowered rug that didn't begin to cover the floor was assisted by a few little scatter rugs with fringe. The slipcovered furniture was the sort, Catty felt sure, that would have been in her illustrated copy of *Little Women*. Velvet-covered, buttoned and tasseled, claw-footed.

"Hey," said Lexy. "What're you doing?"

Catty dropped the skirt of a chintz chair cover. "Testing my wits. I thought this would be very old-timey furniture underneath and I wanted to be sure. I was right. It's like a book."

"You know, there's an awful lot of fireplaces. Even Mom's and Daddy's room has one. I saw when they went in. Not ours, on the third floor, but I bet the second floor has them in all the rooms. There are six chimneys on this house."

"How do you know?"

"I counted them, when we were outside."

"Lex, you are astonishing. The *things* you think to do."

Lexy looked pleased at what he rightly took to be a compliment, but made no attempt to exploit it, which in itself Catty found enviable. She, herself, and despite herself, always tried to extract just a bit more juice from a passing bit of praise. ("Cats, you're a satisfactory small sister; right along the lines I would've chosen." "Am I, Beau? I mean, really? Sometimes I think I talk too much, I mean, I hear my voice going on and on—" "You do, at that. But only sometimes." With a nice laugh.)

"Probably this house was built before central heating," she said to Lexy. "That's why all the fireplaces. They needed them to heat the house. Long ago they probably cooked in them, too. And then came coal stoves, and then those disappeared, and I guess gas and electric stoves will be period pieces pretty soon. It'll all be electronic cooking."

"There aren't any fireplaces in our rooms, yours and mine."

"Those were probably servants' quarters. They'd have had Franklin stoves. Or none at all. And they'd get up at dawn and creep down in the cold to stir up the coal stove and get the porridge going, and then go around lighting fires in the parlors and master bedrooms so when the quality folks arose they wouldn't shiver. That sort of thing. It's all in the books, and maybe the world has progressed some since those days, even if Beau didn't think so."

"He'd have liked those deer."

"Yes."

After a while she said, "Let's look some more."

Behind the parlor was a small room that brightened Catty's spirits. A room lined and stuffed and piled with books. A little library.

"Oh my," she said. "Oh, joy."

Her own books might be weeks arriving, and though she could scarcely have borne to lose them and looked forward with a lover's feeling to their safe arrival here, she eyed this new trove with excitement.

"Boy, what a neat room," said Lexy. "Lookit, Cat. What's that?"

"That, Lexy, *is* a Franklin stove," she said in wonder. "It's what people used in the olden days."

They advanced on it curiously. A large, pot-bellied, black iron stove with polished curly decorations made of nickel. A pipe rose from it, curving in pleats near the ceiling and thrusting out the wall.

Lexy looked around. "There's no central heating in here," he announced. "Uncle Henry must still use that stove, winters."

"I'll be darned."

They sat, each in an old leather chair, and gazed about. It was very quiet. They could hear the grandfather clock in the hallway ticking away the history of the world, and they had a sense, in this room, of having been taken back in that history.

"Maybe George Washington slept here," Catty said suddenly, and they laughed.

"Hey!" said Lexy. "Look at that, will you!"

From the shadowed kneehole under the desk emerged a great gray cat with salmon-gold eyes. He opened his mouth in a protracted yawn and then stretched, one front leg, then the other; then, with care, each hind leg, after which he sat, feet close together, and seemed to ruminate on their presence. His gaze went thoughtfully from one to the other. Catty and Lex, who'd been taught by their brother not to make advances to animals, sat happily still.

"Oh, there you are," said Uncle Henry, coming in. With his chef's hat off he looked even squatter and was, indeed, quite bald, with a snowy fringe. Mr. Pickwick, Catty thought, captivated. "I see you've encountered Huck. A bit long in the tooth, but hale."

Like the guests, thought Catty, fonder by the moment of her great-uncle, who clearly had favorite little sayings and would reuse them without apology.

"How old is he?"

"Fourteen. Rather advanced for a cat, but nothing out of the ordinary. His mother, Clara, lived to be twenty-two. She was here when your brother Beau came on a visit, let's see, that'd be close to fifteen years ago now. He was, Beau was, about four, I'd say. Had this awful allergy to cats, and Clara had to be induced to live in the barn."

"What was Beau like, when he was four?"

"Lively, curious, into everything. Recall his little garden he planted. We planted together, that is. But Beau worked hard at it. He was going to be a farmer in those days."

"What did he grow?"

"Oh, a good respectable garden. Beans, tomatoes, bell peppers, cukes. A regular Farmer McGregor garden, including an overturned flowerpot that he peeked under every morning. He was looking for Peter Rabbit to be there."

"He was like that about animals, even then," Catty mused.

"Oh yes. Beau loved animals all right. Even better than his garden. We had chickens and ducks and a pig or two in those days. He never got tired of feeding them. Talked to them all the time. I swear, I sometimes felt even those chuckle-headed chickens could be reached by the right person."

"Tell me more," Catty begged.

"Let's see—talking all the time, always asking questions—" He broke off as a soft gong sounded from the hallway. "Marian's calling us to supper, children. Shall we go?"

Chapter 13

The guests were assembled in the parlor. With them were Mr. and Mrs. Reed and Virginia. Ginger, who either genuinely liked old people or liked the sense of herself being adorable with them, was surrounded by five old ladies and one old man, beaming on her. The seventh guest was the image of one of Catty's discarded mental pictures of her great-uncle—the strapping ropy fellow fighting age every inch of the way. Except that this old man looked pretty ill-humored, which had not been part of her picture.

"Ah," said Uncle Henry. "Here you all are, getting acquainted, I see. Well, ladies and gentlemen, here are two more members of my family. May I present Catty and Lexy—this is Mr. Hermann," he said, indicating the loner, who scowled at them and then looked pointedly toward the dining room. "Supper in two shakes," said Uncle Henry. "And here in the cluster are Mrs. Armitage, Mrs. Charters, Mrs. Monroe, the Misses Forbush, and Mr. Fell. Shall we go in?"

Mr. Hermann stamped off in the lead and went to a table by himself. The Misses Forbush and Mr. Fell took their obviously accustomed places at one table, the other three guests at another. Near the wall two tables had been put together and were, Catty realized, for the family.

(During the meal, Catty was conscious of the collective gaze and tongue of the guests speculating upon the new arrivals. With the exception, that was, of Mr. Hermann, who kept his eyes on his food, ate with what seemed perseverance rather than pleasure and at the conclusion of the meal left the dining room without a word.)

As they went into the dining room and took their places, Uncle Henry disappeared toward the kitchen, reappeared in his chef's hat, wheeling a cart with a great tureen upon it from which he and Aunt Marian served the chowder, the biscuits, and salad.

"Well, well, well," said Uncle Henry, when he'd seated himself at the head of the family table. "I've been trying to recall when in the past I've been as unreservedly happy as I am today, and for the life of me I can't. I'm sure there've been other times, but for the life of me I can't think of anything but this moment. Upon my word, Amy and Jim, I should have thought to offer you a drink on this momentous occasion. I'm not a drinking man myself, but we have a nice little cellar, and usually on weekends Mr. Fell and most of the ladies indulge before supper. May I offer — "

Mr. Reed held up a staying hand. "Unk. If we wanted something we'd be bold enough to ask, believe me. Come the weekend we'll be glad to indulge with the others. Mr. Hermann a teetotaller?"

They were all talking softly, since at table Mr. Wendell could read lips, and Catty trusted that the loud buzz of conversation from the other tables would obscure their own gossiping.

"My goodness, yes," Uncle Henry was saying in reply to Mr. Reed's question. "Mr. Hermann is a member of a lifetime abstinence group. And not just from the drink, mind. From pleasure." Uncle Henry nodded gravely. "A *lifetime* abstainer from the various forms of pleasure. Mrs. Charters has a membership, too, and, I sometimes think, better credentials. The chief thing about Reginald Hermann is his silence, but Mrs. Charters' chiefest thing is misery. She wears it like a hand knit cardigan."

"Well," said Marian Wendell, "I don't think she can really help it. She has a sort of brooding nature. And Mr. Hermann is shy. Cranky people so often are. Uncle wants everyone in the world to be cheerful all the time just because he is, and things just don't work out that way."

"This soup is great, Uncle Henry," said Lexy. "I never had fish soup before. And your biscuits — like wow!"

Uncle Henry looked gratified and as the meal progressed with noisy good humor and bursts of laughter,

Catty recalled how passionately she and Lexy had wished themselves back in Indiana. And that had been only *last night.*

Funny, she thought. It's a strange, odd, funny, peculiar world, and I'm glad I'm in it. She looked at her sister, whose face seemed unusually serene, and thought, maybe even Ginny's pleased to be here. Of course, if she were asked, she'd shrug or say what difference did it make, she hadn't been consulted and she was here and that was that, and might as well rot here as anywhere else.

"So, what I have in mind, Unk," Mr. Reed was saying, "is to go around the place and look over the things you say need repairing or painting — I've already noticed we're going to have to reroof that barn — and then maybe go into a huddle with this Quincy fellow, to see what ideas he has, and then I'll get to work."

"Get to work at what?" Virginia asked sharply.

"The repairs we need around here. I just said."

"We? Repairs? Do you plan to be a carpenter, Daddy? Or a housepainter?"

"Well in a word, yes. I do."

"You aren't going to look for a job at your own work?"

"Ginny, I don't understand you." Mr. Reed glanced apologetically at Uncle Henry, who listened with interest. "I — that is, your mother and I — told you when we came here that we were going to work with Uncle Henry here, and the work I can do best is — "

"The work you do best," Virginia said, not looking at anyone but her father, "is the work your *profession* fitted you for. You are a professional man, after all."

Mr. Reed caught his lip, started to laugh, stopped, frowned, then said, in an exasperated tone, "There *is* no work for my kind of professional man around here. I told you that men with my kind of qualifications are being laid off all over the country. I thought we'd had this all out."

"It never occurred to me that you seriously weren't going to look for a job, that's all." She lifted her shoulders, let them fall. "However, if you're satisfied to be a handyman — well, that's your problem, isn't it?"

"It's not the only problem I've got, by a long shot."

"I suppose you mean me. I'm a problem."

"At the moment, you sure aren't part of the solution."

"Virginia, Virginia," Mrs. Reed said loudly, then lowered her voice. "Oh, Virginia, *why* do you make things so hard for us? Why can't you try to be — "

"Be what?"

"I don't know. Graceful, maybe. Or grateful," she said with a glance at her uncle, who shook his head disclaiming any wish for gratitude. He didn't, Catty thought, seem at all disturbed by Ginny's outburst.

"All right," said Virginia. "Okay. I guess I didn't actually realize until this minute that Daddy's really given up. That he's going to be a hanger-on, a recipient of kindness, reroofing barns in return for food and lodging for us all, but if that's how it is, all ri — "

"If you were five years younger," Mrs. Reed interrupted shakily, "I'd send you to your room."

Virginia rose. "I think I'll go there anyway." She turned to Uncle Henry. "Sorry I was rude. Sorry, Aunt

Marian. *Thank* you for having us." She walked quickly from the room and up the stairs, leaving the rest of the family and most of the other diners staring after her.

"Uncle Henry, I don't know what to say —" Mrs. Reed began.

Mr. Wendell shook his head again. "No need to say a thing. Except it's a pity such a pretty girl is so discontented. Anybody any idea what's the matter? She really think you've come down a few rungs of the ladder, Jim, by coming here?"

"It appears so. Our daughter, Virginia, is not part of the young generation you hear so much of that scorns material things and status levels. The things of material existence are important to Ginny — not so much *things*, I guess, as appearances. I don't know who's to blame. Amy and I, I guess."

"Parents always blame themselves for everything wrong in their children, I've observed. But they never seem to take any credit for what's creditable. That's always something the kids did on their own. Once in a while, in my lonelier moments, I used to be sorry I hadn't married and had a family, but the more I look around, the less reason I see for regret." He glanced at Lexy and Catty and smiled. "Nothing personal, you understand."

"Heck," said Lexy. "I agree with you. I'm never gonna get married. I'm gonna have a dog and a mynah bird, period."

Mr. Reed burst out laughing and put a hand briefly on his wife's shoulder. "Come on, Amy love. Ginny'll get over her sulk, as she always does. I'm tired of fretting over Virginia. It's marvelous here, just great, and I'm looking forward in a way I can hardly describe to working outdoors, and working with tools, doing something that helps the world instead of researching ways and means of ending it, which, if you come right down to it, was what my job was. I feel as if I'd been reborn here."

"On a lower rung?" she asked, smiling slightly.

"Thoreau would have held, on a higher one. I'll take Thoreau's judgment over Ginny's. She'll come around."

"And if she doesn't?"

"What can we do about it now? If she doesn't change, then she'll continue to be a snob and in a few years be old enough to leave us and begin her upward climb. Look, you get them to a certain age, and hope you've done well, but if you've done the best you know how — that's it. Fini. I've watched too many people totter into old age wringing their hands over where they went wrong with the kiddies. I, for one, am having none of it anymore. I lost my job, I'm starting a new life, you're starting it with me, and we're going to *relish* it."

"What about us?" Catty demanded.

"Oh — I'm still working on you and Lex. Your sister has gotten beyond me, but take it from H.D., he hasn't done with molding your characters yet."

Lexy and Catty listened, watching their father's face with wonder. They hadn't heard him talk like this in so long. Hadn't heard, for months and months, this hearty, laughing tone in his voice.

He's happy, really happy, Catty thought. And Mother

109

is, and I am and Lex is, and Uncle Henry and Aunt Marian certainly are. So that just leaves Ginny, resisting all the way.

She was conscious of relief that she would not, tonight, be required to go to bed in the same room as her sister. Not tonight or any other night. If I don't want to, she thought, I maybe never have to face her bad temper again, always hoping she'll make one of those unaccountable switches and be nice. This is a great big house, and I can just stay out of her way.

"How do we get to school here?" she asked her Aunt Marian.

"On the bus. It comes right by."

"But Ginny will be going to a different school than us. She's a junior in high school this year. I'm going into eighth grade, and Lex will be in third."

"Then you'll all go to different schools. We'll have to find out, get you registered, and whatever else is required. But the bus takes all three of you and lets you off at different places."

I'll sit at the back, Catty told herself. This chance to free herself from Virginia, even though she herself had been the one to cling, seemed to her rather like her father's rebirth — an occasion to rejoice over. She wondered, for a moment, if she'd feel the same when she got up there on the third floor alone in a room at night.

Chapter 14

Mrs. Reed and Catty offered again to help with the dishes when supper was over, but Aunt Marian said that probably Dunc Charters had arrived, and all they'd have to do was get the tables cleared.

When they'd wheeled in the first load, they found a young man perched on a stool at the kitchen table, eating chowder and biscuits. He got to his feet and made a move to take the cart.

"Now, Duncan," said Marian Wendell. "Finish your supper first. Amy, this is Duncan Charters, who works here and we couldn't do without him. You may take that as a threat, Dunc."

"Glad to, Miss Wendell."

"My sister, Mrs. Reed, and her daughter, Catherine — Catty."

Duncan smiled and Catty blinked and thought, I think I just got interested in the opposite sex.

Duncan Charters was long. Extremely tall and lean but not gangly. His brown hair was thick and straight and long, his eyes long and blue—not a cold blue but the blue of the sun on a pond—and his mouth was long, with full lips, and seemed to curve upward at the corners — even when he wasn't smiling.

He had a deep young voice, big hands and feet, Catty could imagine him drinking gallons of milk.

"Are you related to Mrs. Charters out there?" she asked.

"She's my grandmother. I pay part of her tuition, working here."

"Tuition? Oh, I see."

"Duncan comes in here after college every day and helps us out, and that makes it possible for us to keep his grandmother at a very reasonable rate."

Catty found out later that Duncan's parents had been divorced years before, that he had no idea where his father was, that his mother had died a few months earlier, leaving him and his grandmother, who was actually his father's mother, alone. With her social security check, a small insurance policy left by her daughter-in-law, and Duncan's assistance, old Mrs. Charters was able to live and complain here rather than being obliged to go to a state hospital.

Just now, in the kitchen, all she knew about him was that he was in college. *College,* she said to herself. Then it's hopeless.

"But you look about fourteen!" she burst out.

Duncan laughed. "Nineteen, actually. It's a cross to bear, my immature appearance. I don't even get to shave more than twice a week."

"It's a cross some of us would offer to carry for you," Marian Wendell said in a wistful tone. Catty supposed that a lady getting married for the first time at around the age of forty would be sadly conscious of her looks. Even a really groovy lady like Aunt Marian.

"Now that we're positive of Duncan's presence — not that I ever doubt him — shall we go in the library for another cup of coffee? We sometimes sit in the parlor after supper with our friends, but not often. They like to play cards or gossip, and we like to collapse in the library when day is done."

"I'd help Duncan, if I could," Catty said hesitantly.

"Yeah. Me, too," Lexy offered.

"I'm sure he'd be delighted. Don't forget to throw out the scraps for the racoons, Dunc. The children are dying to see them."

The children, Catty said to herself mournfully, looking at Duncan, who already had ceased to appear fourteen.

Their mother came up to the third floor with them that night. She saw Lexy tucked in, then came into Catty's room and sat in the wing chair.

"I won't stay a moment," she said, yawning. "It's been an incredibly long day. Would you believe that this morning we were still at that motel?"

"I know. I thought of it before."

"You like it here already, don't you?" said Mrs. Reed.

"Oh, Mom!"

"I'm so glad. Your father does, too. I've always liked this house, this part of the world. I've missed it."

"Did you notice that Daddy called himself H.D. tonight?"

"Wasn't it marvelous?"

"*Virginia* was horrible."

"I just don't feel like talking about Virginia at the moment," Mrs. Reed said, sounding troubled nonetheless.

But Catty was agreeable. She lay propped up in bed, looking around the room with peaceful pleasure. On the bureau was a little blue lamp with a six-sided shade showing scenes of a city.

"That's an old sperm-whale oil lamp," said Mrs. Reed. "Converted to electricity. I can't remember when it wasn't around the house someplace. I'm glad Marian put it up here for you. Those scenes are of Paris, in the late nineteenth century."

"I love it."

At that moment, the door, which had been nearly closed, was thrust open and in walked Huck, looking about with easy self-assurance. He hesitated, studying the room, and then with an air of decision, leaped onto Catty's bed and settled down to wash.

"I guess you aren't going to be alone up here, at that," said Mrs. Reed.

Catty put a gentle hand on the big cat's round head. "He's friendly, isn't he? Coming all the way up here to keep me company. Do you think he'll stay?"

"Who knows? He looks as if he were settling for the night. Seems to me he came looking for you."

"Do you really think so?" Catty felt a small rush of jealousy. "Look out and see if Lexy's door is open."

Mrs. Reed checked. "It is. So it was you that Huck was after. I guess he recognizes a cat lover who's always been waiting to have a cat."

They were silent a moment, looking into the past, and then Mrs. Reed rose. "Sleep well, both of you. I'll leave the little lamp on." A quick kiss and she was gone.

Catty lay listening to the rain which had begun while she and Lexy watched the racoons, and now was pelting heavily on the roof, rushing through a rainspout somewhere nearby. The air coming in gusts through her open windows was fresh-smelling, grassy. In the distance thunder growled lazily.

With the purring musical bulk of Huck beside her and the lamp glowing softly on the bureau, Catty lay and listened, unafraid, even a little thrilled, to the roll of thunder in the night.

How darling the racoons had been! Fat and solid in their rough fur, with keen masked faces and long-fingered black paws. There'd been a mother and three babies, and they'd come shambling out of the bushes when Duncan called.

"Hey, you guys," Duncan had said, tossing fish heads and tails onto the grass. "Chow time."

A rustling in the dark, and then the racoon family humped into view, easy to see in the light that fell from over the kitchen door. They'd moved cautiously up to the fish scraps, and with unhurried, almost dainty, motions began to eat.

"Oh, gee," Lexy kept saying, his eyes wide with delight. "Oh, golly. Lookit that, Catty. *Look* at them."

"I am looking."

But she knew what he meant. Presented with such bliss, it was almost as if they couldn't look hard enough, as if their senses were not equal to the joy of what they saw. She'd felt the same watching the deer. And yet it seemed that now, in this place, she and Lex would be able to see animals in their freedom, lots of animals. Duncan said there were foxes in the hills and that sometimes you heard them bark, and once in a rare while he had seen one running along the stone wall that descended from the hilltop to the road. Uncle Henry owned two hundred and fifty acres and except for mowing the meadow and cutting down an occasional dead tree for firewood, he did not allow those acres to be tampered with. Not hunted or fished on, or sprayed with things, or improved in any fashion.

"He just lets it be," Duncan had said. "What grows, grows. What falls down, stays there. What gets eaten by birds or animals, gets eaten. All the gardening is done organically."

"What does that mean?" Lex asked.

"No insecticides or weed killers or growth encouragers, except for compost, of course. Mr. Wendell dotes on his compost heap. But he's a man for letting Nature have her way. He fences in the vegetable garden, but that's all the protection they get—the vegetables, I mean. The people who drown everything they grow in sprays would be surprised how good things taste that are just let grow. A bit bitten, maybe, and not always shapely, but *good*."

"You sound like our brother, Beau," Lexy said. "That's the way Beau used to talk."

"Used to?" Duncan had said curiously, and Lexy, who'd had a long and tiring and happy and exciting day, burst into tears.

I wonder, Catty thought now, her eyelids drooping, if we'll get over crying, suddenly, without warning, because Beau is gone. She did not, just now, feel like crying herself. She felt at peace. At peace with this day, with Beau's dear memory, with Huck's sleeping companionship. She thought she could hear an owl hooting somewhere in the trees in the falling rain. But of course she didn't really know what an owl sounded like.

Chapter 15

Tending the plants in the overfoliated bay window, Mrs. Charters fetched up a sigh so profound that Catty, who'd been trying to slip past unseen, felt summoned. She moved reluctantly to the old woman's side.

French cane within reach, Mrs. Charters was removing mealy bugs from the Christmas cactus. She used a cotton swab dipped in a bottle of rubbing alcohol.

"Doesn't do to let them get ahead of you," she explained querulously. "A scourge, bad as aphids. I take care of the houseplants, you know. Gives me something to do and makes me feel that something, even if it's only a plant, needs me."

"They're beautiful, Mrs. Charters. I mean, no dust or anything on them. We had some plants at home but they always died."

She hoped her mother, who took good care of plants, wouldn't hear her, and wondered at the same time why she felt this need to propitiate old people, even with lies. Virginia had told her once that it was patronizing and she rather thought Virginia was right, but continued to do it.

As so often happened, it seemed to work with Mrs. Charters, who said with a disciplinary air, "If you permitted them to get clogged with house dust, then no wonder. A plant must be bathed or its pores close up, same as a person's, and then it can't breathe and it naturally dies, what else is there for it to do? Of course, no matter what care one takes of them, at some point a plant is just too old and useless to be worth saving. That one, for instance." She stabbed the air, delivering judgment on one of the many pots.

"What is it?"

"A cyclamen. Past rescue. Like me. Like most of the old crocks in this place. Except we do a better job with plants and animals than we do with human beings. No dumping *me* in the compost heap to moulder and decay and eventually nourish. Oh, no — I'm to drag on, leafless, unsound, jeopardizing the young lives around me, an onus to them, dependent on the mercy of a boy who lets me *know* I'm dependent, never fear — "

"Oh, my goodness, Mrs. Charters," Catty exclaimed. She moved awkwardly, nearly upset the alcohol, grabbed at the bottle to steady it and knocked a floweret off a geranium. "Oh, my — I'm sorry."

"It's all right." With an air of pessimism, justified, the old woman studied the geranium. "Leggy, isn't it? Suppose we take it down to the basement and let it rest for a while. Hibernate, as it were. Except, since this is summer, we'll have to say estivate, won't we?"

"Estivate?" Catty said with pleasure.

"A long summer sleep is estivation, as opposed to a long winter's sleep, hibernation."

"I didn't know that."

"Well, there you are. A new fact. I must say, you seem an unusual child. Today's youth doesn't listen to the old. As if all we'd learned and lived through had no bearing on life, no value for anyone. It's a shame, I tell you, a shame." Her voice rose, trembling. "What are we to do? Kill ourselves? All the stored-up knowledge of a lifetime and it's pushed aside like a ten-cent toy. Do you know I have to get down on my knees even to get that grandson of mine to come and *talk* to me once in a while? I'm at the end of my life and I'm *alone*. I always knew I'd end up a lonely old woman in a room."

Oh misery, thought Catty. How did I get into this? "There're all these people — " she began.

"I tell you I am alone. Unwanted. You'll find one day that you can be lonelier in a crowd than in an empty room."

I've read it often enough, Catty thought. So maybe it's true. "Mrs. Charters, I'll have to be — "

"We'll take that plant to the basement."

Mrs. Charters took her French cane and rose, looking quite dignified.

"Where're you two going?" Aunt Marian asked, coming downstairs with an armload of linen. "Dunc and I are changing the beds," she explained to Catty, who hadn't asked.

"See what I mean?" old Mrs. Charters said in a voice more shrill than feeble. "See? I *am* a burden."

"Oh, I'm sure he doesn't think that," Catty said nervously.

"A burden. If he didn't have me to think of, that young fellow would be out gamboling with his chums, not here doing *female* chores." She made the word female sound unseemly, second-rate.

Without a backward glance, Mrs. Charters started up the stairs, pausing now and then to wave her cane angrily. She disappeared down the second floor hall.

Catty, the geranium clutched against her chest, looked at Aunt Marian. "She said we were going to put this leggy geranium in the basement to estivate."

"Better put it back. This isn't the time of year to give a geranium time off. It's all right," she said, noticing Catty's hesitation. "She won't remember."

"What a pity about her. I mean, she's *interesting*, but she's so awfully unhappy."

"Well, it *is* a pity, but we've never been able to figure out what to do about it, so we've given up trying to do anything."

"Could I help you?"

"All right. Put the plant away, and then you can load the machine while I fold."

"Does Duncan really change beds?" Catty asked, when they were working side by side in the laundry room.

"Why not? It's a job that needs doing. Are you in

agreement with his Granny that men are above certain kinds of work?"

"I guess not," Catty said uncertainly. Her father had never made a bed or done a dish in his life, she was sure. Nor had Beau. But Duncan Charters cheerfully went about this so-called woman's work and seemed none the worse for it. His grandmother was clearly the better for it.

Duncan had a room off the kitchen, and once Catty had had a glimpse of it when he'd forgotten to close the door. Totally disordered. The bed looking as if it had never been made, piles of books and papers and pamphlets everywhere, clothes tossed about. Even as she'd looked, something, a slight breeze, a settling of the floor, had dislodged a stack of paperbacks that slithered gently against another stack and upset it. Duncan obviously felt that housekeeping stopped at his door, and Catty, who would have loved to tidy his room for him, at the same time didn't dare offer.

"What's Duncan going to be, when he gets out of school?"

"He's a science major, that's all I know."

"Where does he stand with the draft?"

"His lottery number is pretty high. But in any case, he says he wouldn't go."

"How would he get out of it?"

"Oh, he says there are any number of ways and he'd find one. Of course, I think it's all academic in his case, because he really is his grandmother's sole support, except for her little income. But that isn't the point. It's that there are so many young men like Duncan, who just will not be turned into killers. Get enough of them all over the world and maybe one day the miracle will happen and men will actually stop killing one another."

"Beau said there would always be men ready to send other men to war, and they'd always find men willing to go. Like in that poem about the average citizen — *When there was peace, he was for peace, and when there was war, he went.*"

"Beau was a Marine. I suppose most of them think that way."

Catty looked at her aunt with surprise. "Didn't Mom or Daddy tell you about Beau? How he refused to fight any more? I mean, he was a Marine, all right, and he volunteered, but he — Oh, Aunt Marian, he *changed his mind*. He changed it altogether. Didn't they *tell* you that?"

"They never speak of Beau at all. You're the only one who does."

Catty looked around the kitchen for something to rest her eyes on until the familiar pricking at her eyes, the danger of tears, passed. She looked through the laundry-room door at the big wooden-framed clock and the kitchen wall. Ten thirteen.

At ten sixteen, Duncan came in with a large paper sack of litter from the upstairs wastebaskets. "I don't know what the end of all this is going to be," he complained. "Every week there's more trash that can't be destroyed in *any* way. Look at all these little plastic wrappings, will you. It's gotten so they wrap everything but new-born infants in plastic, and it may come to that yet."

123

"Can't you burn them?" Catty asked.

"All this burning up of practically indestructible junk that we use to encase our mountains of stupid purchases is going to end by blotting out the sun entirely. One tiny little planet and we're systematically drowning it in crud. Probably one day we'll start shooting it all into space and contrive to pollute the entire universe."

"Then what's the answer?"

"I'm not sure there is any, except not using the damn stuff."

Catty sighed. "You and Beau would have been *such* good friends."

"Tell us about him," Duncan Charters said. Catty gave him a piteous look. "Don't you want to?"

"Oh, I do. I really do." She swallowed. "It's just that I can't always keep from — from crying. I mean, sometimes if I talk about him I don't, but usually I do. Except I don't often talk about him. None of us talks about him."

"Why not?"

Catty shook her head. "I've never been able to find out why. I guess Mom and Daddy can't, except I think I loved him as much as they did and *I* want to. Ginger just looks over my head and waits for me to finish if I start saying anything. And Lex is too young, really. He has this way of — of not seeming to know that Beau is dead."

"Well, I have to clean the oven in the kitchen there, so why don't you tell me as much as you feel like telling?"

Catty glanced at her aunt, who said, "We'd like that,

Catty. I only knew Beau as a very little boy. An enchanting little boy. I'd like to find out something of what he grew up thinking and believing."

Catty drew a deep shaken breath. "I'll have to get my Keeping Box. It has some pictures of him. And some letters."

Chapter 16

The earliest letter was not a letter at all. It was a scrap of paper on which Beau, who must then have been around Lexy's age, had written, *I Love Mommy and boiled pudding.* Catty had found it in a book one day in the spring and had taken it to her mother.

"Oh, Mother, *look* at this. You must have tucked it in *Bleak House* years ago. Why is it so touching, when it ought just to be sort of funny?"

Mrs. Reed had glanced at the paper and turned away, seeming nearly to bend over, as if warding off a terrible ache.

"Mother, I'm sorry!" Catty had cried out. "I didn't know it would — I'm *sorry!*"

After that, she stopped, almost entirely, speaking of Beau. She told no one how often she dreamed of him —

that he was alive, so that waking was like losing him again and again. She told no one how often she cried out, sometimes silently, sometimes, if she were sure she could not be heard, aloud — "Come back, Beau, please. Oh, come back!"

She joined the silence that was not forgetfulness and suffered there with her mother and father and possibly Ginger, and maybe, in his way, Lexy.

"Ah, gee," said Duncan, reading the little scrawled note, "I can see how a thing like this would break a parent up. It gets to me, even, and I never knew him at all."

Catty rummaged among her snapshots, selected one of her favorites. Beau on a bike, aged about ten, looking at the camera with a grin for his father who was taking the picture. A bird feeder dangled over his head from the one tree they'd had in their yard, and a chickadee seemed to be leaning over to look at the boy as if knowing this was not one to be feared.

"Good-looking, wasn't he?" Duncan said.

"Oh, yes. Beautiful. He looked like Percy Bysshe Shelley, except not at all ethereal. Here's his high-school graduation picture. I don't like it as much. He looks as if he took himself awfully seriously, and really he didn't."

"Oh, I don't know," said Dunc, studying the smooth and formal young face. "We all have to take ourselves seriously in some way, and there's nothing like a year-book picture to capture the emotion. A solemn time, you know. Threshold, future, great world, all that. Do you have the yearbook itself?"

"It's with my books, if they ever get here."

"Did they have those little sayings, quick character analyses that so often hit the nail on the head?"

"Oh, yes. And all the things you did in school. Beau was president of the student body, and president of the Nature Club, and captain of the basketball team, and manager of the swimming team, and he belonged to the Spanish Club and the Thespians, and the Senior Mixed Chorus, and he was on the varsity track team and varsity tennis. They said his outstanding characteristic was 'Talks Least, Says Most,' and the quotation was *I am a Part of all that I have Met*."

"Good God," said Duncan.

"Oh, I know," Catty said with hurt defensiveness. "You think he sounds like some sort of square, don't you?"

"I do not. I'm impressed. Really impressed. That's a range of interests and activities that would have to make an interesting person."

Catty studied his face for signs of sarcasm, but saw none.

"He did have a lot of interests. Sometimes you got the feeling that there wasn't anything Beau wasn't curious about. I mean, lots of times Ginny says she's bored, but I never heard Beau say that. Not once." She brooded a moment. "He didn't like people very much."

"How's that?"

"I mean — human beings. Homo sapiens. He said the species was a failure and we'd have to evolve something better or resign the world to destruction. He had friends, and he loved us, and all. But not the human race. He loved animals, of course."

"Better than people?"

"I suppose so. I think I do, too. Animals don't hurt each other. Not deliberately. People do it all the time."

"Look, Catty," Duncan began hesitantly. "There's one thing I don't understand about your brother — "

"You want to know how he ended up a Marine."

"Well, isn't it strange? Doesn't it seem out of character for a fellow who was like this, who, as you say, cared so deeply about the fate of the world, who read a lot and thought a lot, and according to all this he certainly did — uh — " He ran a hand through his hair. "Forgot what I started out to say."

"No, you didn't. You think someone like that wouldn't volunteer to go to war and kill. Well, Beau didn't. Not that way. He was — in addition to all *these* things —" She gestured at the high-school photograph and what it represented " — he was kind of wild and nervy, I guess you'd say. Not jumpy. I mean, his nerves were acute, very easily touched, you know? Well — he and this friend of his, Sam, went canoeing up in Canada, and what happened was there was an accident and Sam drowned and Beau didn't, and some people sort of suggested — not really said, just made Beau feel — or he only *imagined* it, but either way it came out the same — that he — " She paused and closed her eyes. "That *Beau* had somehow let Sam down, let him drown. That Beau was a coward," she finished wearily.

There was silence. She opened her eyes and looked at Duncan, who regarded her steadily.

In a moment she said, "Beau was wise and wonderful, but he wasn't absolutely grown-up, and he wasn't im-

pervious to stupid people's horrible innuendos. So I
guess he ran off to be a Marine to show he wasn't a
coward and all he showed was how stupid he could be.
For such a dumb stupid reason he went off and got himself killed. But I don't think when he went he was thinking about the part where *he* killed. I just don't think he
thought at all, until it was too late."

Listlessly, she selected a few letters from the box.
"Here are these, if you want to read them." She gave
them to her aunt, who read them one after the other,
handing them to Duncan. While they read, Catty sat
motionless, looking at the big clock.

". . . a sergeant who could've been reading a manual
entitled *How To Be a Sadistic Sergeant Like in the
Flicks.* He's mean clear through. Mean-spirited, mean-
tempered, with mean little eyes and a mean squeaky
voice and probably a mean little childhood in back of it
all but that doesn't help us much. I hate the guy so that
it's dissolving my insides. I'm getting to be a hollow
thing filled with hatred. Nobody needs to tell me I
shouldn't feel this way or write this way, I know I
shouldn't. I got myself into the mess and should shut
up. Only I can't shut up — except maybe I'll work on
trying to and maybe I won't send this — "

But he had, in fact, sent it, from the boot camp in
Virginia.

". . . it's difficult to decide what or how or how often
to write, since I realize perfectly well that my letters are
one long yell of self-pity, and boy, do I pity myself and

130

every other one of us in this platoon because we're CRETINS who got ourselves into this hell with our little brittle feelings getting hurt, or some such matter, so we can't even say we got drafted. *For round me the men will be lying/That learned me the way to behave,/And showed me the business of dying,/Oh who would not sleep with the brave?* Well, I for one, would not. I'd rather go home. Listen, Serious Sisters, if you two ever grow up (joke) and they start conscripting women, take a tip from H.B. and don't carry Housman into battle. He dilutes the martial spirit. I'd advise Kipling, or maybe that gorgeous St. Crispin's Day speech by single-minded Harry of the soaring tongue and the creeping I.Q. While I'm being literary (and isn't this a literary letter?) I recall that Thoreau called self-pity the most brutal of all emotions. Maybe brutal situations bring it out. This South Vietnam is very pretty country, or probably was except that we're rapidly making it ugly past believing. But would you have guessed that it could be a beautiful country? I never would have, from anything I've heard or been told. From where I'm sitting I can see across some fields to a ridge of purple mountains — there's a little village over there that looks as if it were woven into the trees. The people, especially the women, are beautiful, beautiful — "

And another, later one.

". . . no, no, no, Mom — you've got it all wrong. I *don't* have gonorrhea. What I said in that letter was that the lieutenant gave us all a lecture on V.D. practically as soon as we got off the chopper. With posters and big easy letters and short easy words, just like in hygiene classes in junior high. How the heck could I have gonorrhea? I haven't even had a leave yet."

Duncan gave a snort of laughter. Catty had included that letter wondering if he would. Her father had thought it was funny, too.

And the last one.

". . . I wish I could write, and think, more clearly than I do. I know you all hate this war and protest it when you can. But you can't know or hate it the way we do. I mean, except for a few cro-magnons we've got here who can't see farther than the next chance to 'pick off a gook.' This isn't any sort of reproach of you, because how *could* you know. You're there hating it, we're here doing it. And what's happened to me, all of a sudden, or maybe not so all of a sudden — is that I *will not go on killing.* I've killed a couple of men, and yesterday I killed a kid. A kid. A child. A boy. Some of these V.C. here are twelve or fourteen years old. Mine looked to me about Lexy's age. I'm really sick. I mean to my stomach, to my head, I think I'm sick to my soul. I went to the lieutenant today and told him I'm not going to load my rifle anymore and if it comes to killing or being killed well then I lose and he could do what he wanted to about it. Now look, family, my people I love, don't go up in smoke, because it's all going to come out roses — so quit worrying. In this squirrely world it often works out, I guess, that an act that sounds maybe courageous (morally, anyway) turns out to *be* an out and that, by golly, is what I got for myself without intending it at all. If I'd known it was this easy, maybe I'd have done it sooner. I mean, they're

132

sending me to a psycho hospital, in Saigon or Okinawa. I'm not sure yet. I'll go out tonight on the medical chopper, disgraced in some eyes, a hero in some, and I don't give a damn either way. The deal is the lieutenant thinks I've lost my marbles so they're shipping me off to a shrink to see if they can get me back into combat-readiness. (Hah!) If the head doctor can't locate the old marbles and talk me into being a good soldier Schweik again, I'll probably get a psychiatric discharge, and never be able to get a job except spiking litter in a park. But I'll be out of here. Maybe I'm a bit squirrely at that. I mean, reverence for life can be carried too far, can't it? There's a mosquito on my arm, about the size of a baby bomber, and I can't bring myself even to kill him. Next letter from the hospital. Oh, boy — clean sheets and a bed!"

"And then?" Duncan asked, handing the letters back to her.

Catty smoothed each one and gently laid them back in the Keeping Box.

"Then an hour later he crawled across the field to try to pull a boy with two shot-up legs out of the line of fire and back to their bunker. They were both killed. Beau got a medal. I mean we got it. That's in here, too. Do you want to see it?"

Aunt Marian shook her head, and Duncan said, "No. I guess not."

Catty stood up, holding the Keeping Box. She looked at the clock again. Nearly half-past eleven. "You didn't get to clean the stove, Dunc."

"That's all right. You didn't cry."

133

"I didn't, did I?" She sighed. "Thank you both. I — needed to talk about him. To have somebody else know about him. I guess I'll take this back upstairs."

In her room she leaned on the windowsill and thought, I'll be looking for Beau all the rest of my life, and I've always known that since he died. What she hadn't known was that she'd find him, once in a while, in an unexpected way, as she'd found him in Duncan's partisan eyes, in Aunt Marian's gentle attention.

Chapter 17

Catty, with Huck lying on the grass a few feet away, was swinging on the swing in the front yard. Its radius was small and she continually had to push, in the deep worn place under her feet, to keep it going. It was late dusk. In the house there were lights on in the parlor, the library, and at some of the upstairs windows. Virginia's second-story room was lighted, and Mr. Hermann's. Virginia would be up there reading or listening to her radio. Catty had no idea what Mr. Hermann did when he was alone in his room, which was most of the time. Her own small high window glowed softly with the light from the little lamp.

She loved to do this — to be outside in the gathering dark, looking in at lighted windows, as if at a stage, seeing the furniture inside, and the pictures on the wall,

and an occasional person moving in a silent world unaware of her watchfulness. It was a cozy, contented sen-
sation, a feeling that, even in summer, spoke of hearth
fires, of security and love.

As she shoved, first with one foot, then with the other,
and leaned against the ropes, listening to their sturdy
and ancient protest against the huge branch above, she
saw Mr. Hermann come to his window and stand, looking out. She waved, and in a moment, he waved back,
then disappeared. She knew what expression would be on
his face. A stone-quiet look she no longer took for cranki-
ness only, but also for a vast shyness that occasionally
cracked, permitting a quick smile, or, as now, a brief
signal before he submerged again.

In the parlor, although she couldn't see them for the
plants at the bay window, Mr. Fell and three of the
ladies — Miss Anna Forbush, Miss Nell Forbush, and
Mrs. Augustus Monroe ("I'm Professor Monroe's relict,"
she had said to Catty, who could scarcely believe her
ears) would be seated at the round table playing bridge.
Mrs. Armitage and Mrs. Charters were also invisible,
but Catty knew they were in there; Mrs. Armitage knitting and appearing to listen while Mrs. Charters talked
continuously, aimlessly, unstoppably, interrupting herself, back-tracking, surging on, lifting her voice to ward
off interruptions, reminiscing, speculating, complaining,
blaming herself for errors committed long ago, for the
death of plants improperly tended, for living too long,
for living at all. Mrs. Armitage, who appeared to practice
patience and charity on Mrs. Charters, would be nodding

136

her head from time to time in what might be either agreement or drowsiness.

In the library, she could see Uncle Henry and her father at the big desk, going over plans for various house repairs now under way, like the painting of the barn and house trim. Her mother was talking with Aunt Marian and Mr. John Grimmett, lately arrived from a business trip to Canada. He and Aunt Marian were to be married in a couple of weeks. Catty dreamily looked forward to the wedding.

"Tell me about how you met," she'd asked her Aunt. "I love stories about how people meet. I mean, people who are going to live happily ever after. Did you know Mom and Daddy met at a fund-raising dinner for a Democratic congressman who lost the election by twenty-seven votes?"

"Oh, yes," Aunt Marian had laughed. "We all know about that."

"It's terrible, when you come to think of it — how chancy things are. I mean, suppose one of them hadn't gone to the dinner, or had been a Republican or something?"

"Then you wouldn't be here, would you?"

"Well, that's what I wonder sometimes. If Mom had married somebody else, who would I be? Somebody else? Part of myself? And *if* I was part of myself, which part would it be?" She'd hugged her arms and gave a half laugh.

"But all life leans on this sort of chance, so if it were not this way it would be some other way, just as random.

It's all a fortune wheel. If you think about it enough, you might come to think that none of it matters very much anyway," Aunt Marian had mused. "Since it could easily have been some other way. Some other person born, having different experiences, but experiences, just the same — quite as important to him."

But what Catty meant was that *this* person, herself, not part of some other or some other entirely, but Catherine Reed *as she was,* had had to be, and it was unthinkable, terrifying, to realize she might not have been, save for that Democratic dinner. It was too overweening and too self-important an idea to share with Aunt Marian, so she'd asked again how she and Mr. Grimmett, a pleasant, big, fair-haired man that everybody liked, had happened to meet.

"Ordinarily enough. Accidentally enough. At a faculty dinner given by a friend of mine in the English department at the college. John is her brother, and he was here from California, and she invited me to even out the table."

"How romantic," Catty sighed. "You read about those dinners where the table gets evened out, but mostly I guess the people just carry on a conversation until coffee and dessert and then think thank heaven *that's* over. But you and Mr. Grimmett fell in love."

What a nice expression it was. So headlong.

"John and I — " Aunt Marian had paused, her pretty face kindled with an inward, excluding joy. "John and I," she said again, "fell in love. I thought it would never happen to me, to have somebody out of the whole world matter more than the whole world — " Catty had moved uncomfortably and Aunt Marian broke off, flushing.

You wanted to know things about them, about adults, Catty thought. But not too much. Not terribly personal particulars. A sentimental gauze about Aunt Marian was lovely, but not a glimpse behind the veil. The truth was that in spite of words like "falling in love," in spite of her parents' obvious affection for each other, and Mr. Grimmett's clear doting on Aunt Marian, Catty could not believe that adults really felt things keenly. Not, oh not at all, the way young people did. How could they?

Well, not to think about it. Anyway, in no detail. It was wonderful to know they had a world of their own in which to be happy but it had to be a happiness different in kind from the absolutely penetrating, mind-swinging, heart-stopping joy that young people, and especially children, could know for no reason at all. She wasn't sure that she now, at thirteen, felt the flashing mindless bliss that Lexy still knew at times. Perhaps not knowing why — perhaps that *was* the why of young rapture — so much of the present, with no thought for how it had come or when it would go. Now she knew it would pass.

"Children and animals," Beau had said once, "are the luckiest creatures on earth in one way. They live *now*. Children don't rehearse for life, and animals don't prepare for death. Everything is now."

"That's awfully good, Beau. Who said it?"

"I said it."

"I mean, who said it first?"

"Me. Just now. I've often thought it, but only just said it now."

"It sounds profound."

"Maybe it is. I think it's true. I remember, when I was a kid, just tearing off down the street on my bike could make me so wild with joy I'd yell like a banshee. *Yeeeowww!* No reason. I wasn't going anyplace or planning anything or getting anything. I just felt good, great, *glorious*. Oh, to be a kid again."

"Or an animal?"

"That'd be okay, too, provided I wasn't somebody's watchdog or a trained seal. Anything free, even if it ended up being gunned down. To be free while it lasts, that's all any animal wants. Free and alive *now,* that's happiness."

I can remember feeling like that, Catty thought, swinging slower and slower, finally stopping, arms high on the ropes, leaning back, brooding. I remember feeling — enraptured — for no reason at all in the world.

Because I remember, does that mean I'm not a child anymore?

She jumped up and ran indoors, Huck following with his rocking-horse gait, and burst into the parlor.

"That child always comes into a room like something thrown through the window," Miss Anna Forbush said to her sister, Nell, who nodded eager agreement. Like Uncle Henry, the Misses Forbush were hard of hearing. Unlike him, they did not read lips, and always spoke as if their hearers were as deaf as they were. "Can't think what the Wendells are up to, letting a family with children into the Inn. We were led to believe that this would be a quiet, well-run establishment."

"These are their *own* family, Anna," Nell informed

140

her, and the rest of the room as well. "I've told you that, dear."

"Oh, yes. Well, there's nothing they can do about that. Family's family, when all's said and done. That older girl, the pretty one, is quite nice. But this one's awfully noticeable. And there's a *boy*, too," Anna said gravely.

Catty's face burned and she began to back through the doorway, but Mr. Fell, calmly dealing cards, winked at her. Mrs. Monroe, the relict of the professor, said softly, "Pay no mind, Catherine. They aren't accustomed to young people, poor things." She raised her voice. "Your bid, Nell."

Mrs. Armitage, cornered, as Catty had supposed she'd be, by Mrs. Charters, said, "Come here, child. Sit with us, won't you?" She made it sound an appeal, so Catty, trying to walk quietly, went to them and perched on an ottoman.

"You really mustn't take what the sisters say to heart," Mrs. Armitage observed, patting her knee. "As Fanny says, they aren't used to youth. We should just be sorry for them."

"They like Ginger."

"Well, she has a soothing way of behaving with the elderly. A mixture of condescension and pity, as if we weren't quite all there, you know."

"Is that soothing?"

"I think so. Being treated like a mental deficient puts so little strain on one. Oh dear, that's tactless of me. Virginia is truly very sweet to all of us. She has a natural gift for getting along with old people, and it's quite wrong-minded of me to wonder why. And naturally, anyone so young and vital might feel a sense of superiority toward age."

"I don't," Catty said, bluntly and truthfully.

"You aren't as young as Virginia."

"But I — " Catty broke off, suspecting she'd been paid a compliment but not altogether sure.

Mrs. Charters, who'd followed this exchange with unaccustomed attentiveness, now interrupted peevishly, "The young of today feel no respect for age. When I was a girl, my parents saw to it that we respected them. A sign of disrespect and Father took the rod to us, girls though we were. I remember one time my sister, Meg, tried to take the part of the Suffragettes — not that she *marched* or did anything unseemly or unladylike but she did feel, as she said, I can hear it as if it were yesterday, that maybe if women had the vote they could work for the good of mankind, and I remember she even said *womankind,* too. Meg was very advanced, and Father turned the whole roast upside down on the table, it put him in such a state, and sent Meg to her room for a week. You don't see anything like that *these* days, I'll bet a cookie — "

"I didn't see anything like it in those days," said Mrs. Armitage, looking at her aged companion with a sorrowful expression. "What happened to Meg?"

"Nothing. Nothing ever happened to her, except she died young. Only in her forties. Never did marry, but I don't think it was so much that she became a feminist — not that she ever did anything unladylike, mind, she just took to the Cause . . . I couldn't see it myself and I can't see that anyone's any better off since women *got* the vote . . . no, it was more, I believe, that no one ever asked her. Can't say she seemed to mind, she said women with husbands and children thought they'd fulfilled their destiny but actually all they'd fulfilled was some man's, or else why weren't they happier? She was always after me about being happy, but I'm just not by nature a happy person. I mean to say, you see all these people smirking around and laughing and pretending to be happy but I ask you, how many of them really are?"

"Some, I hope," said Mrs. Armitage.

"No, I didn't really hold with all that woman's emancipation myself, but it never made Father like me better for agreeing with him. He was angry about evolution, too."

"Angry about it?"

"Father always said that no one in his family, or anyone he *knew* either, was descended from something that was half rat, half monkey, and half fish. That's what he said, and to this day I agree with him."

Three halves, thought Catty. Isn't that beautiful? She looked at Mrs. Armitage, who put down her knitting in order to laugh unimpeded. Catty took the opportunity to jump to her feet and claim to be needed in the kitchen.

There she found her sister sitting on a kitchen stool, elbows on her knees, chin on her fists, burnished hair falling to either side of her face, watching Duncan. To Catty she seemed to resemble some long-legged lovely bird. A flamingo, maybe.

"Oh, I suppose I'm getting to like it well enough," Ginger was saying. "Except it seems so horribly far away."

"From what?" asked Duncan.

"From intellectual stimulation," said Ginny.

"Thanks a bunch."

"Oh, Dunc. I don't mean you. You're brilliant, of course, but you're never here to speak of and when you are you're slaving." She sighed. "Oh well, I guess I mean there doesn't seem to be much *fun.* And no young people. Except you. Slaving, as noted." She turned, saw Catty, smiled. "Hello, lambie. Come along in and join us. We're doing up, as I think the saying goes."

Catty, taking a dish towel to help dry, couldn't help but admire Virginia's calm assumption that whatever role she chose to play, people in the family would go along. Now she was going to be a darling older sister, so Catty would be the darling little sister, and, actually, what else was there to do?

If she said, "Oh knock it off, Ginny, an hour ago you told me I was a boring little pest whose only future was probably to be a zoo keeper" (not, Catty added to herself, that I'd *mind* being a zoo keeper), but if she said that, then Virginia would lean over and ruffle her hair and say, "Little love, you know I was only worrying about your obsession with that moribund chipmunk. I want to you to be a *girl,* not an animal behaviorist."

In one economical gesture, she'd make Catty look unfeminine and about eight years old, and herself tenderly mature.

"Where does the double boiler go?" she snapped.

"There, in that closet with the other pots," said Duncan. "Say, you sound sort of tired, Catty. You don't have to do this."

I wasn't tired a minute ago, Catty thought fiercely. It's an effect my adorable sister has on me.

"You do sound sort of whiney, love, and it isn't *like* you, unless you're exhausted. Why don't you run along to bed? Lex went ages ago."

"Because I'm not Lexy's age, and I'll decide for myself when I want to go to bed, that's why."

"Well, of *course*. We're only too happy to have you here. It's just that Duncan and I both noticed — "

"Oh, blah," said Catty, throwing the towel on the table and walking out the kitchen door. She stamped off to the barn. A lamp over the great door picked out a chiaroscuro scene within. A small tractor — to mow the meadow and plow the snow, Uncle Henry had said — a haystack, sweet-smelling, kept by Uncle Henry who had a barn and no horse for a neighbor who had a horse and no barn — a row of empty stalls — some snowshoes and skis hanging on the wall — and over in one corner a big screened box where the chipmunk she'd rescued from Huck was living until it recovered from shock and a wound on its side.

The little thing scampered a bit when she reached in for it, but then lay quietly enough in her hand while she applied some ointment Uncle Henry had given her. Not moribund, or even close, anymore. It seemed really chirpy when she put it back. Probably tomorrow she could release it, and then it would have a little more time to tunnel along the meadow wall and nibble whatever it found to nibble and brighten the eye with its striped flash of tiny vehement life, before Huck or some other animal got it.

A shadow fell beside her on the barn floor, and she looked up to see Duncan.

"You startled me."

"Sorry. I was emptying the garbage and thought I'd come over and see if there's something wrong. You hurled out of there so suddenly, I thought maybe you were sick or something."

"Or something," said Catty, glancing toward the kitchen, where she could see Ginny, still perched on the kitchen stool, confidently awaiting the return of her admirer.

If Duncan was her admirer. It was difficult to tell.

"How's the chipmunk?" he asked, stooping down to look.

"He'll recover. Maybe I'll let him go tomorrow."

"Good." He straightened. "Have to get back and finish up. You okay, Cats?"

She nodded, and after he'd gone sat for a long while in the hay-smelling half-dark beside her patient, who rustled in the straw bed she'd made for him, and now and then sat up, paws against his white chest, to look at her.

Chapter 18

Mr. Reed had nearly finished the job of painting all the wood trim on the big brick house, and most of the great barn besides. When Catty realized that he meant to do this job all alone, she'd been astounded. How could one man with two hands set himself such a task? But her father went at it with gusto, scraping, priming, painting, whistling, growing browner and cheerier as the days passed.

He frequently had Lex to help. Lexy was grave and precise about responsibilities, and could be relied upon to do a careful job of window sashes which, his father assured him, was about the trickiest bit of all.

Lexy, his steady hand moving over countless narrow bands of wood, nodded. "I like this kind of window best," he said. "This kind with all the little panes,

147

instead of just one big one. Or two. These look like books. People singing Christmas carols in the books are always in front of windows like this, all piled up with snow."

"Well, this is a Revolutionary era house, and that's how they made windows in those days. Couldn't make sheets of glass as strong as we can."

In the week before the wedding, when it looked as if the barn might not be completed on time ("probably I'll have only the back left to do," Mr. Reed said one evening, "but I wish I could've got it all done, so that the wedding guests would not be dazzled just by our facade") Mr. Fell had offered his help. For the final days, then, before the important day, the three of them worked together. Catty found it an altogether fetching sight. One brush vigorous, one shaky but game, and one severely meticulous. Among the three of them they got the barn painted without harm to the row of steepling hollyhocks that stood inches away from it.

One way and another the whole complement of the inn was drawn into preparations for the wedding, except for Mr. Hermann who emerged from his room only at mealtimes, and Mrs. Charters, who was everywhere, bitterly reproachful and apologetic at being in the way.

The Misses Forbush turned out to have a knack for polishing brass, and under their ministrations fireplace tools, fenders, bowls, doorknobs, door knocker, took on a satiny sheen they had not had, Aunt Marian declared, for years. "Sadly neglected," she said. "And now just look at them!"

Anna and Nell Forbush beamed and bridled.

They probably, Catty thought, don't get complimented very often, don't often feel they've accomplished anything. She told herself that she would, really truly would, try to be nicer with them, pay attention to them, care about how they felt and what they did. Not only the Forbush sisters, but all the other guests. Mr. Hermann, too. And — yes, and Mrs. Charters. It was easy enough to be agreeable with Mrs. Armitage, or Mrs. Monroe, or Mr. Fell. Mrs. Charters was the challenge Ginger was apparently equal to. In, it was true, an elusive, "some-other-time-I'd-love-to-hear-about-it" manner. Who was she to criticize Ginger for insincerity? How did she even know Ginger was insincere in her role of being exquisitely kind to the old?

Well, I *do* know, Catty said to herself stubbornly. It's like when she was a candy striper in the hospital, looking absolutely darling in her tight-waisted pink uniform, the little pink cap like a butterfly on her hair. She'd looked, as she was repeatedly told, "as pretty as the flowers she carried," going about the wards and rooms with ginger ale and bouquets and a tender sort of hovering air all the while seeing herself doing it, and seeing the young interns seeing her do it. That had been after Sam, when Ginny had said she had to find something to *do,* to take her mind off all that she had lost, though she'd lost Sam months before he died, and she wasn't fooling anyone but herself about that.

After she'd dated three or four interns, with not many repeat dates, Ginger had given up hospital work. "Interferes with my school work," she'd said sharply to Catty's query. "Besides, sick people have a funny smell."

149

The old people in the inn here didn't have a funny smell. Mr. Hermann and Mr. Fell were crisp and cologned, even though Mr. Fell's tie was usually spotted with something he'd dropped while eating, his old hands being unreliable. The ladies, every one, were immaculate. It was a good audience on which to project a sweet-girl image.

When she found herself thinking like this, Catty experienced a puzzled self-reproach. What's the matter with me? she'd think. What kind of a sister, what kind of a person, am I? Jealous and small-spirited and mean. Oh, how she envied sisters who loved each other. She had to admit that mostly she found them in books, those girls whose thoughts intermingled humorously, lovingly, who stood together against the world and had secrets and shared and sacrificed for each other. They were to be found most often in the works of English women writers. There was usually one sister, the eldest, who was beautiful and chic and knowing her own mind, and the other who was dreamy and bookish and plain but, you were implicitly assured, would grow into her own specialized sort of lettered beauty. Catty wistfully supposed that all those women writers had known such relationships as girls. But although over the years she and Ginger had made a few attempts to become that kind of sister, it had never come to anything but embarrassment.

Nonetheless, where the old people were concerned, Catty condemned herself as a greater hypocrite than Ginger when, after a few advances to the old guests, she relapsed into inattentive courtesy because, except for

Mrs. Armitage, they bored her. Ginger, at least, and whether or not she was sincere, gave pleasure.

But during the final week before the wedding it had not been difficult to be forthcoming and easy, because everybody was doing something (except Mrs. Charters and Mr. Hermann) and that made for easy relationships.

"We're like one big happy family, aren't we?" said Mrs. Monroe, and Catty thought that for once the sort of silly-sounding expression had merit. It was like a family affair. Meals at the inn became sketchy as days were spent making casseroles, and hundreds of canapes to be frozen ahead of time. There were to be two huge fruit-studded hams and two great turkeys and melon balls in white wine. There was to be champagne.

And the cake — oh, the cake.

Uncle Henry made it. It was four-tiered and covered with candied rosebuds. Candied, Catty was astonished to find, by Uncle Henry himself.

She had sat watching him brush the young buds and leaves with egg white, using a little sable-tipped paint brush as delicately as a Japanese artist. This process was followed by a faint but thorough dusting with powdered sugar and then the roses had been dried in a very slow oven for twenty-four hours. When this many-colored mass of frosty sculptured flowers and leaves had finally been arranged, the day before the wedding, on the high white cake, Catty looked at her great-uncle with awe. He was a lovely, dear, and good man, and she knew that better every day.

"But I didn't know you were an artist," she breathed,

151

and though she spoke so softly he could not have heard a word he knew what she had said and pleasure creased his plump ancient face.

Even Virginia had been wonder-struck.

"Good heavens," she said to Catty. *"That's* what he's been working up to. It's — it's a prodigy of beauty. It's a love poem. Do you eat those rosebuds and leaves, do you suppose? I mean, *does* one? Not that one would."

"I think it's a pity to eat it at all. It should be put under glass, like a Victorian bouquet."

Mrs. Armitage came into the kitchen, a big apron around her ample middle. In common with the others, this week of activity seemed to have put a new lightness in her step, a new glow in her eyes.

"Thought we'd get at the melon balls, girls." She stopped, her mouth dropping open, staring at the cake. "I declare. I do declare. I've never seen its equal. Heavens knows, I've seen many a bridal cake in my day, but never one like this before." Arms folded, she gazed at it. "Tell you what—before we start on the melons, would one of you run up and ask the Forbush ladies and Mrs. Charters if they'd like to see it before we put it away? Mr. Wendell says we're to hide it in the wine cellar, but I do think they should all have a chance to share."

"I'll do it," Catty offered.

She went through the dining room and parlor, up the narrow stairs, thinking how now all was familiar that had been so strange not so very long ago. Now this was home. The worn runner on the stairs with brass rods newly gleaming, the cheval glass murkily reflecting her figure, the odor of mustiness, lemon-wax, and all the various products that people sprayed on themselves and their possessions these days. This long hallway was home.

Past Mrs. Armitage's room, past Mr. Fell's and Mr. Hermann's, and so to the Forbushes'. She knocked softly, then harder, getting no answer. Debating, she risked gently opening the door to peer in. The room was crammed and crowded and crushed with furniture, with bric-a-brac, with *things*. Like a barn sale.

For a moment, the clutter and chaos so confused her that she mistook the two figures on the backless bench at the window for another part of the decor, and then became aware that the sisters were sitting there, silent in their deafness, having no need when together to cope with the complexities of their earphones which tended, in company, to fail them, or to utter high shrill squeals. The Misses Forbush had a bizarre manner of diving into their bosoms to adjust their hearing aids, and seemed to go on a presumption of invisibility when so engaged. It sometimes caused surprise in onlookers.

But there they were, backs to her, unaware of her. Binoculars on the windowsill among the African violets showed that perhaps they'd been bird-watching. Catty thought that she could offer to do that with them sometime. She liked bird-watching. Probably Lex would enjoy it too. If we just made an effort, she told herself. A real *effort*. You can't just tell yourself people are old cranks or bores and ignore them because you don't feel like being bored.

She was, she *was* going to be different.

There they were, and what was it about their thin, stoop-shouldered silence, their immobility before the window that made so sorrowful a picture? Because they seemed, though together, so alone? Because they were holding hands? They were. Not looking at each other, not speaking, not moving at all. Just sitting side by side, hands clasped, waiting for something.

Why did a glimpse like this of two people who, after all, might just be peacefully staring out the window, cause her pain?

The little quick smile Mr. Fell sent around the table when his trembling hand had once again betrayed him, leaving a spot on his vest. The sight she'd had once of an alley cat, bone-skinny, patiently trying to wash his matted, his hopelessly grimy fur. The little boy she'd seen that time on television, when a kind man had taken some blind children to the Children's Zoo in Central Park in New York City. "Now, children, here's a baby lamb. Who would like to touch it?" "Oh, I would," the little boy had said, holding his hands in front of him, turning his tumble-haired head from side to side. And, after a little pause, "Please, where is it?" Catty had burst into the sort of sobs that strangled, that tore at the throat.

And oh, she had wept for the Little Mermaid, for the Highwayman and the Harp-Weaver, for Oliver and Little Nell, for Charlotte the spider, for the nightingale that sang her life away, breast crushed against the thorn. She had wept for Jo, the crossing sweep boy, and for Beth and Bambi, and for that great Grizzly. Still today she had only to recall the last lines. . . . *and he lay down as softly as he had in his mother's arms in the Grey Bull long ago.* They hurt, they hurt — words like "long ago."

Her English teacher in school last year, a teacher she had never liked, had surveyed his class one day in a way he assumed when he was going to let them in on an adult angle of something that had seemed until then a straightforward matter without angles. "Somebody — I guess it would have to be Oscar Wilde — said that a man would have to have a heart of stone not to laugh at the death of Little Nell. So, you see, your *attitudes* will change as you get older and what may twist your heart at one age may very well turn your stomach at another."

Catty had sat very still, thinking, my attitude toward you wouldn't change if I died at age one hundred.

Now she inched into the Forbushes' room uncertainly, not wishing to startle them, but wanting very much to call them out of their motionless soundless world.

"Miss Anna! Miss Nell!"

It was their preference to be addressed in this manner, and every time she did so, Catty felt like one of the March sisters.

"Miss Anna! Miss Nell!" she said again, wondering if anyone ever said, "Miss Nell! Miss Anna!"

She tried, and, oddly, it secured their attention. They turned to her with identical little gasps, with a shared air of vagrant bewilderment.

155

"We thought you might like to look at the wedding cake before we hide it so Aunt Marian and Mr. Grimmett won't see. It's beautiful."

They rose with alacrity, faces eager, company manners donned in an instant. Like a pair of big birds they set up a chatter, then swooped across the room and out and down toward the wedding cake.

I must have imagined it, Catty said to herself, going across the hall to summon Mrs. Charters. People aren't melancholy and pining, the way I think. I just think along those lines too much. Or read. They didn't feel alone and abandoned at all. Having reassured herself, she knocked briskly on Mrs. Charters' door and delivered her message, escaping before the net of Mrs. Charters' conversation could whine through the air and drop over her.

Later, when the cake was concealed in the wine cellar and the prospective bride and groom warned not to descend, Ginger and Catty helped Mrs. Armitage and Mrs. Monroe to make hundreds of melon balls. As they mounted glistening in a great wooden bowl, little nearly perfect spheres of coral, of pale pungent green, of sparkling crimson, the air filled with fragrance. Inside each melon half, the scoopers took away rounds, leaving thin-waisted flat-topped columns of fruit that they spooned into another bowl for the racoons, now and then stealing some.

"Catty," Mrs. Armitage said into a peaceful silence touched only by the ponderous tick of the big wall clock, and by occasional lazy siesta calls from birds outside, "Catty, love. Go to the garden and get us some mint, will you? We'll wash it and keep it in water, and tomorrow there will be nothing to do but garnish. We must leave as little as possible to do tomorrow."

In the garden, crouched on the grass, was Lexy, absentmindedly plucking raspberries from a bush, eating with leisurely savor as he studied a bee, a great black and yellow velour bee with trailing legs, that hovered around the enticing berry bushes.

"Hello, darling," said Catty, feeling, maybe because the day was so happy, or maybe because he often affected her that way, a melting tenderness toward this sober-sided fellow, her brother. "Nature observation?"

"Sort of. I was wondering—Cats, do you suppose a bee has a tiny little heart?"

"Why, I never thought about it. I suppose he'd have to have."

"But think how little bitty it must be," Lexy said, obviously fascinated by the attempt to reduce his vision to the scale of a bee's heart. "Think of it, beating there in his chest. Does a bee have a chest?"

"Oh, Lex!" Catty burst out laughing. "Oh, Alexander, I do love you."

"Mmm," said Lexy. But he didn't look displeased.

Chapter 19

The eve of the wedding.

On impulse, on her way to the third floor, Catty stopped and knocked at Ginger's door.

"Come in!"

A pin-curl cap, beribboned, bebowed, concealing her hair, Ginny sat at her dressing table, giving herself a manicure. Her face was covered with a pale beautifying mask.

"You look like Marcel Marceau," said Catty, droping to a chair. "Yuck."

"Ah, but wait until the butterfly sheds it chrysalis, you won't yuck then."

"I believe you."

Catty looked around the room, and realized how Ginger must have suffered, living double. Her own room was neat enough, but aside from her books she had in no way embellished it since she arrived, except to make the bed in the morning.

But here there was exhaled a perfume of young female beauty. Ginny's room, like all those on this floor, had a fireplace, and above the mantel she had put a framed fan, of peach-colored ostrich feathers and tortoise shell.

"Where did you get that?"

"Mrs. Monroe gave it to me. Isn't it super?"

"Gorgeous." Was that a twinge of envy? No — on thinking it over, definitely no. She would never wear or display the feathers or fur of creatures. Which did not mean the fan wasn't exquisite. "Where did you get all this stuff?" She waved at the dotted swiss bedspread and the bolster pillow covered with a dotted swiss sham, at the silken soft canary-yellow throw folded at the foot of the bed, at the lusterware vase in which Ginger had arranged dark blue petunias striped with white, with pink gypsophila clouding around them. The effect of the room, in the lamplight, was golden and white, with just that streak of vivid blue in the flowers to lend a touch of dash.

"Naturally good taste," Catty muttered. "Wonder how a person comes by it."

"Well, as you just said — naturally."

"Meaning I couldn't acquire it?"

"Who said you don't have taste? You have your own

kind. Everybody can't be like me," Ginger said, sounding genuinely sorry.

Catty laughed and looked around the room again. Me-first Virginia had a way with things, all right. It was a puzzle that a person so comely, so brainy, so endowed with the goodies of life should put people off with such perfect regularity.

If we were really friends, or friends at all, I could say to her, Look, Ginny, isn't it about time you look into yourself and try to find out what the matter is? Maybe if you got a single other interest besides the one you already have, you'd be able to start moving into that world you're always talking of — the world of intellectual stimulation and interesting people.

She couldn't say that to this Ginger, painstakingly attending to her appearance, seemingly confident that that was all she need do. Poor girl, Catty thought, and was at once astonished at herself. Had she ever before said to herself in such a merciful, motherly — no, sisterly — way, *poor girl,* about Virginia, and meant it? No, she had not.

She wished she could say something aloud, to indicate to her sister without putting it into words that might constrain or embarrass them, that she was here to listen, to help if she could, that she knew Virginia couldn't really be happy, walled off in her conscious superiority to other people.

"Ginny," she said urgently, "could I help you? Is there some way *I* could help?"

"With what? You might better be upstairs attending to yourself. Aren't you going to wash your hair? It looks stringy, dear, and you want to look your best tomorrow, don't you? What are you wearing, the yellow or the pink? I," she said, going to her closet, reaching cautiously as her nails might not yet be fully dry, "am wearing this!"

She held her dress aloft, with a flourish of joy — an apple-green cotton, high at the neck, narrow to the hips, flaring in a tulip swirl at the hem. A beautiful dress, properly adored by its owner.

"Did you know," Ginger went on, beginning her pedicure, "that Mrs. Monroe is making Aunt Marian a little hat all of real nasturtiums? Pale yellows with a few orange-colored blossoms for emphasis. Aunt Marian's suit is a sort of tangerine silk, or not really silk, but you know — "

Looking at the masked face lifted queerly as Ginny reached for the nail polish, Catty could see behind the forehead where her sister had a picture of herself, young and lithe and golden-brown in the apple-green dress, long hair unadorned and shining like mahogany, eyes sparkling—simply taking the show away from the middle-aged bride in her mastershallum hat.

She got up.

"You going?" Ginny asked. "Well, I have to get this mask off pretty soon. Hope I don't run into either of the old gents in the hall and give them cardiac arrest. You really should wash your hair, love."

"Yeah. 'Night, Ginny."

But Ginger had bent over her toes again and apparently didn't hear because there was no response.

In her room, Catty found Huck curled on the bed.

161

He looked up at her entrance and mewed a lazy greeting.

"Happy to see you, too," Catty said absently. She stood looking around, as for something mislaid.

Her books had come and were arranged in a case provided from some other room by Uncle Henry. Her eyes rested on them fondly. They'd always, probably, smell faintly charred, but here they were, where they belonged at last. The fairy tales, the complete Jane Austen in half-calf (an expensive Christmas present of two years back) her Dickens and Stevenson and Brontës, and those newer books by modern marvels like Krutch, and Loren Eiseley and Josephine Johnson. Her poetry —all the way back to *Silver Pennies. Nymph, nymph, what are your beads? Green glass, goblin. . .* Yes, the spell of the words lingered.

She ran a gentle hand along the spines of these battered companions, without whom — what? Without whom, unthinkable.

Still her eyes wandered. All at once she went to the closet for her Keeping Box.

Long ago, until Beau had gone to boot camp and even for a little thereafter, she had kept a commonplace book. She got it now from the bottom of the box and took it to her chair, switching on the lamp beside her, sitting with the volume unopened on her lap for a while. In there were lines of prose and poetry gathered from everywhere for sustenance when she should need it.

Without checking the last entry, she turned to a new page and wrote, *Do not grieve, or keep me always in your thoughts, but think of me as you would remember a book you loved in childhood.* Simone Weil.

It was absolutely the only line in the book by Simone Weil she'd tried to read that she had understood, and this line she understood as if she had written it herself.

Chapter 20

A knock on the door. Huck looked up with calm interest, closed his eyes again as Mrs. Reed came in.

"Thought I'd visit for a few minutes, all right?"

"I'd love it. Aren't you exhausted? You've worked for a week without stopping."

"It's been fun. I'm going to miss Marian. I feel as if we've wasted so much time."

"I still wonder why two sisters who loved each other would make so little effort to be together all these years."

"Maybe because—we didn't know we loved each other."

"But you used to say — "

Her mother shrugged a little. "There's no way to explain that either, except I guess I told you in order to tell myself that we'd been close. I wanted to think we'd been."

Catty understood that.

"Well, I think it's sad," she said, "for you and Aunt Marian to discover each other just as you're about to fly apart."

She looked up to find her mother's eyes fixed steadily and curiously on her face.

"Why are you looking at me that way?"

"Oh . . . just wondering what goes on behind that forehead. I often look at my children and wonder, *What's in there? What are they thinking?*"

"I was thinking about being kind, about being a really good person. I want to be, you know. It's just that I get bored so easily with people who are boring, and that's *wrong* of me. I mean, even a bore needs some kindness, wouldn't you say? Look how nice Mrs. Armitage is to Mrs. Charters. And then the Forbush sisters this afternoon. They looked so awfully lonely. And I was wondering if you shouldn't — I mean, if *one* shouldn't — try to help people out of their loneliness. I guess I'm not making sense."

"Oh, yes. It's sense, but perhaps it isn't possible. Loneliness as a situation can sometimes be corrected, but as a state of mind it's incurable, like anxiety. You just have to settle down and live with it. And I believe all people get lonelier as they get older. Perhaps it's a blessing — a way of learning to withdraw from life."

"I never thought of that."

"I suppose it's not a child's perception."

They looked at each other, then smiled, because in spite of their wistful words they were happy.

"Just the same," said Catty, "I have miles to go before I'm nice."

"No, you haven't," said her mother, as Catty had known she would. "You're quite — nice now. And a few other things, like adorable."

Catty sighed. "Can I get by without washing my hair? Would it look all right tomorrow? Ginny says it's stringy."

"Wash it in the morning. The wedding's not till four."

"Have you seen Ginny?"

"Oh my, yes. She'll steal the scene."

"That's exactly what I thought. I mean, I thought that's what she was thinking." She reflected a moment. "Not consciously, I suppose."

Mrs. Reed yawned. "You know, Cats — something just occurred to me. You don't chew your hair any more."

"I know."

The last time had been at that motel, when she'd gone to sleep with a hunk of the stuff in her mouth. "How do parents put up with children?"

"And how do children put up with parents?"

Catty smiled dreamily. What a lovely day it had been, and tomorrow would be better. "Mom, do you think I've changed, sort of? I mean, aside from hair-chewing. Giving *that* up. Have I changed? Grown some?"

"A great deal. Your father and I have both noticed."

166

"Then why didn't you say something?"

"Why? You'd still have changed, and grown. Besides, parents don't tell their children they're growing up, because then they'd be obliged to admit it's true."

"Is it sad, seeing your children grow up?"

"I suppose I should say it isn't, Catty, to spare your brooding over your father and me. But it is sad. Sometimes I think it's the most poignant emotion a person ever feels — remembering that child, seeing this adult. *Where in the world have the children vanished?* Even the poet didn't know."

"I'm not an adult."

"Well on your way, well on your way. Besides, you know what I'm trying to say. It involves those words you yourself always say are so sad — *Once upon a time. Long ago.* For the parent, it isn't so much that you, yourself, are growing older, as that that child, that child that you *knew,* is gone. I look at you and I see a little girl I once knew and she's as lost to me as . . . as Beau is. Oh, dear — " Mrs. Reed wiped her eyes. "Sorry, Cats."

"I don't see why you should be sorry for crying," Catty said gravely. "I cry, sometimes."

"Do you, dear? Well, tonight we mustn't cry anymore. There's a wedding tomorrow and Marian's happiness to think of, and besides — think how much sadder I should be if you *weren't* growing up."

"I wish," Catty said without thinking, "that Beau were here." She gave her mother a quick, apologetic look. "Sorry, Mom."

167

Mrs. Reed leaned her head against the chair back and closed her eyes. "I wish Beau were here, too. I wish it all — no, not all the time — sometimes, for a time, I forget. Do you?"

Catty nodded. But she thought she didn't, not really. She thought that the consciousness of Beau, the awareness of his absence, was always with her. But maybe not, maybe she had times of relinquishing him, but didn't recognize them.

"I think," Mrs. Reed said in a pained, musing voice, "of that poet he loved so, that I dislike so. Housman. There are some lines of his that stay in my mind, and will not go away. Oh, to develop what Ginger calls instant erase."

"What are the lines, Mom?"

A pause, and then her mother's voice, quite steady, quite without expression:

> *"I know not if it rains, my love,*
> *In the land where you do lie;*
> *And oh, so sound you sleep, my love,*
> *You know no more than I."*

She put a hand over her mouth, remaining motionless for some minutes, while Catty lay still and did not cry. And then with a swift motion, Mrs. Reed was on her feet, and smiling.

"Now — to sleep, dear Catty. Tomorrow is going to be a wonderful day, full of happiness, and we'll tell ourselves that Beau is just someplace else, which he is. We've said that before, haven't we? Good-night, my lovely daughter."

Catty gazed at her mother with wonder. You tell yourself that people just aren't demonstrative. You even, because you're too young and wrapped up in yourself to notice what they're feeling, tell yourself that they aren't feeling anything at all.

"Mom!"

Mrs. Reed turned.

"Could I use your electric hair-curler tomorrow after I wash my hair? I thought I might try to make some of those Brontë-type ringlets they show on television."

Mrs. Reed laughed, and with an air of sharing a watchword, said, "Feel free."

She was gone.

As long as she wasn't washing her hair, Catty decided not to bother with her face or teeth either. She put on her nightie, went across the hall to the bathroom briefly, returned and got into bed. Huck, as if on a signal, burrowed under the light blanket and settled at her feet, like a lion cub at a crusader's boots.

For a long time she lay, hands behind her head, listening to the night sounds. The persistent, querulous note of the whippoorwill, the occasional hoot of an owl (and she knew now what an owl sounded like), proclamations from bullfrogs in the pond across the road and cricket choirs in the deep dark grass. A mild night wind lifted the curtains at her windows.

So, gradually, gradually, they would come to speak of Beau. And did that mean he was closer to them? Or that they had, at length, agreed to believe he was gone?

"Feel free," Beau had used to say. If somebody said could they use his bike or his football, could they get a ride downtown with him, or tell him their troubles, Beau would always say, "Feel free."

So Catty said now, aloud, "If you want to haunt me, Beau, why — feel free."

Because, of course, he always did.

Chapter 21

It was the morning of the wedding. Catty, an early riser since she'd come to Vermont, crept down the stairs at dawn and out into the garden, where long wooden tables had been set up on sawhorses, and folding chairs, to be put out later, were stacked just inside the barn.

To the west, across the valley, the land was folded still in semidarkness, and here and there a light shone at the window of some early risers. Though, for that matter, thought Catty, there are not really late risers in Vermont at all.

To the east was the meadow that topped the hill and then fell away and rose again as forest. As she watched, Catty saw the round top of the sun rouge the leafy branches and above them the sky lose its pallor in the limest of greens. Above that was blue to the farthest reaches, and the morning star was still nobly steady in all this advancing light.

"Oh, beautiful," she whispered. "You're so beautiful."

"That's a great place for skiing," Uncle Henry had told her, his eyes on the long slope of the meadow. "And sledding and tobogganing."

"It snows a lot here, doesn't it?"

"A lot. Come Christmas, you and Lexy and I will go up there, to the woods, and get us a tree for the parlor."

"Oh, Uncle Henry!"

In her mind, she had clothed this landscape in white. She saw a shoveled path between the kitchen and the barn. The street outside and the driveway would be cleared, but everywhere else snow would be thick and unthreatened. At home it was so quickly plowed and leveled and dirtied that the only joy they took in it was while it was falling. But here there would be months of unsullied fields and forests lying beneath drifts and expanses ever higher, only marked by ski trails and sled lines crossing and recrossing, and, come Christmas, the branchy pattern of a tree dragged along the snow from the forest to the parlor.

She thought of silent, furry drifts piling up the windowpanes, up the sloping barn roof. On all the bare branches of trees now in full leaf would be ropes of snow, like cotton, so that the landscape became a tracery of white and black lines. She thought of snowmen, big and sturdy as football players, lasting for weeks with their frozen carrot noses pointing toward the sky. Lex and I will build the biggest snowman we've ever seen, she thought, and realized that she meant to be here in the winter, in the snow, in the springtime of thawing and the coming of peepers, and forsythia like scrambled eggs on all those green bushes near the wall. She meant to be here in the summer to follow and all the time to follow.

This is where I want to be, forever.

As she walked into the walled garden on the heavily dewed grass, an indigo bunting flew from a dogwood tree and up over the rim of the meadow, a flash of purple beauty. Overhead, a blue jay was caroling his morning bell-sound.

The wall of the garden was built of seasoned bricks on which time had put an apricot tinge, and over it clambered a clematis bush with blossoms big as saucers that were beautiful by day and addled the senses on a moonlit night with their gleaming china beauty. Oh, the flowers in this garden—the names of which she was learning from Aunt Marian. Hollyhocks and snapdragons and nasturtiums she would have known, and those five giantesses at the corner of the barn—sunflowers lifting their huge heads almost to the eaves.

Here, in this garden, were salpiglossis, astilbe, gypsophila, delphinium, lupine, foxglove, stock, candytuft, columbine, sweet William and verbena and forget-me-nots, and what was lovelier, their names or themselves? And there were roses, in a bed darkly mulched with coffee ground and edged with white alyssum. What names *they* had. Peace, and Carrousel and Sutter's Gold and Madrigal. Talisman and Mojave and Fire King and

Eclipse. Some were named for people. Helen Traubel, Christian Dior, Betty Prior.

"What do you think," said Virginia, suddenly beside her and Catty hadn't heard her coming, "whatever do you imagine Cecile Brunner did or was, that she should have a rose named for her?"

Catty shook her head. "I can't think."

"I believe that to have a rose named after me I would give up nearly everything that people aspire to. Fame, jewelry, voyages, men mad for the touch of my hand — all of it. To have a rose named after me . . . what heaven."

"You look like a rose," Catty said, surprising them both.

And indeed, in her short pink housecoat, fresh and ruffled, with her long glossy hair and long glossy legs and immaculate, faintly flushed complexion, Ginger did put her sister in mind of a bud on its slender stem.

"I wish we got along," Virginia said, looking not at Catty but up toward the meadow where a low morning mist that had shrouded wall and bushes and long meadow grass was curling and sidling away under the now-risen sun that slanted down through oaks and pines in bars of light, like the illustrations in a child's Bible.

I wish we did, too, thought Catty, but couldn't say it. For weeks Ginger had been sullen and withdrawn, and now in one of her swift about-turns was appealing for forgiveness, or for understanding, or maybe for love. But I don't move as quickly as she does, Catty thought. I can't forget that easily and go from one emotion to another as if they were rooms with no doors between.

174

"What sort of rose would you want to be?" she asked, a halfway step toward meeting her sister's need.

Ginny's eyes went over the rose garden, but she didn't have to ponder. "One like Aquarius. Prettier, if possible, but that would do." Pure, vivid, fragrant, with thick pink curling petals and a deep heart and almost no thorns. "Which would you be, Cats? No, I'll tell you. You'd be like Madrigal." Two-colored blossoms, lemony shading into orange, tart and sweet and thorny. Only I don't think I'm the thorny one, Catty said to herself.

"How come you're up so early?" Catty asked, as Ginger said, "How's your chipmunk?"

"I got bored staying in bed —"

"I let him go a couple of days ago —"

They eyed each other, then Catty said, "How could you be bored when you aren't even awake?"

"But I am awake."

"I mean, not usually. It isn't even six o'clock yet." Virginia was the one who lay abed mornings now, refusing to face the days.

"I was thinking about the wedding. You'd think they'd have had one of those marvelous striped tents. With a lawn this big they could've had a really splendid one. That little dance floor looks so *little,* doesn't it?"

The workmen had brought the dance floor, about twelve feet square, in a truck the day before and set it off to the side. A three-piece string orchestra was to sit on chairs on the grass and play during the reception, after the ceremony at the church on the green.

"When I get married," Ginger said, "I'm going to have a pink striped tent and a rock band."

"Something old, something new," Catty murmured and thought that in her way Ginger was reassuring, because you didn't have to wonder where you were with her. You were neck-deep in Ginger's interests, that's where you were. Naturally, on Aunt Marian's wedding day Ginger was thinking about her own.

"What's that look on your face about?" Ginny demanded.

"I was thinking — remembering the Harrisons. How Kitty Harrison had to have this enormous big wedding and her father took out a loan to pay for it and three years later hadn't paid it back and meanwhile Kitty and her husband were so poor they had to move in with the Harrisons with all their expensive wedding presents packed in eighty-four cartons in the attic and everybody got along so horribly that by the time the wedding *was* paid for, Kitty and her husband were getting a divorce."

"So that's what you were thinking," Ginger said sweetly.

"Yup."

"The implication being that that's what I'll do to Daddy."

"With a pink striped tent and a rock band, he'll be more than three years paying."

Virginia shrugged. "Actually, I don't think I'll ever get married at all. Not unless I get out of Vermont, I won't. Who could anybody marry in Vermont? I've never seen such a state. People apparently get born here and then kill time until they die. Now why are you laughing?"

"Oh, Ginny. At you, of course. In the first place, you've only seen two states anyway. Here and Indiana. And you haven't met very many people in Vermont, have you?"

"I certainly haven't."

"Well, but whose fault is that? You refuse to go anywhere. If you'd come to that church supper with us last week —"

"Church supper!" Virginia looked about in despair. "I want life, and you offer me a church supper."

"It was fun. And there were plenty of interesting people there, too. Boys from the college, for one thing. Friends of Duncan's, who are going to summer school, too. He says they go to the church suppers because the food is always great, and it was. And some of us played Twenty Questions, and that was great. I mean, I kept wishing you'd been there, because I've never known anyone better than you at Twenty Questions, you could've held your own with the college kids, and I'd have been proud of you and you *would* have had fun, whether you think so or not. There was one boy with a guitar who sang and he was fabulous. So you missed all that."

"Huh."

"Ginny, I don't understand you. You're always saying you want life and intellectual stimulation and all that, but you hole up in your room reading and won't talk to anyone but the old ladies. Not that you aren't a proper treat for them, but what are they for you?"

"They make me feel wanted."

"Oh, the poor little match girl."

"Sometimes to be a poor little match girl is the only open option."

"What about Dunc?" Catty said boldly. "You seemed taken enough with him at first."

"Oh, Miss Snoop? I rather thought you were the taken one. You follow around after him making gasping sounds all the time."

"I dote on him," Catty said evenly. "But he is, after all, an older man. Just the age for you, if you get what I mean."

"I do, and you bore me. Furthermore, he bores me. He's a hippie loafer, that's what he is."

"Oh, for Pete's sake, what a dumb remark. He's not a hippie because he'd like to see the Pentagon taken down stone by stone. Anyone with brains or a heart in this country feels that way. And he's not a hippie loafer because his hair is long. It's beautiful hair. And he certainly is not a loafer. I never saw anyone work so hard. At school nearly all day and then —"

"Then chop-chop back to the scullery. I know. I suppose all this chambermaiding is hard on him, but it's scarcely the background to make a man compellingly attractive."

Catty turned away. Why did Ginger always disappoint her? Or why did she go on expecting, against most of the evidence, that Virginia would change into a sister out of a book? Out of, Catty added honestly to herself, a book of my choosing? Maybe Ginger was a character out of somebody else's book and maybe she herself had better start accepting that.

The sun was up now, and Virginia gone back in the house, saying over her shoulder, "Put some *clothes* on, Catty. You aren't a *child* anymore, you know." Catty took one last look around at this country she'd come to feel part of, at the hills and meadows lying serenely under the early light, at the just-to-be-seen steeple spiking through far off trees of the church where Aunt Marian would marry her man today. I adore this, she thought passionately. I'll be living here all my life. I *have* to live here all my life. Her gaze went slowly, lovingly over the landscape, where even the telephone poles with their looping wires somehow seemed right, with a tenure not as ancient as that of the trees, but true and touching, and speaking of a human need for closeness.

She was shaken all at once with an utter, dizzying joy, so that she lifted on her bare toes, stretching her arms above her head, and barely restrained a yell of ecstasy — the sort of meaningless pagan shout that Beau on his bicycle might have given years before.

Then, with one last glance toward the top of the meadow where the deer might have been, but were not, she turned toward the house. As Ginger had indicated, she was in her short nightie, which wasn't absolutely opaque, and it wouldn't do to shock the old ladies and gentlemen, either with exhibition of joy or with her nightclothes.

Duncan was at his window, smiling at her. Catty's eyes dropped. She had an impulse to make a dash for the door but then just simply stood, looking back at him.

He moved his head from side to side, as if in wonder.

"What a lovely creature you are, Catty. And what a pity that I'm too old for you, or that we aren't in another century where I wouldn't be. We just missed each other."

Catty's head swam, meeting his blue, rather dazed eyes. She could feel the thick pulsing of her blood, and her heart thudded against her breast — unmoored again. "You could wait for me," she said in a low voice.

"Maybe I will," he said. And then, with an attempt at a laugh, "Maybe I will, at that." But his voice was shaken and he moved back into his room abruptly so that something fell over and broke.

He's smashed a cup or something, Catty said to herself. She went to her room in a trance, trembling faintly, feeling miraculous.

Brightness fall through the air. . . .

Like a barely awakened sleepwalker, she stood looking around, swaying slightly. Everything was subtly altered, strange — the room, the furniture, the view from the window, her body in the light gown, and her image in the dim mirror as she moved before it and confronted herself.

Is this, she wondered, searching her own eyes, studying closely her slender neck, her young breasts faintly discernible through the nightgown, her herony legs, is this what Ginger has done all these years before a mirror? Not looked at herself. Looked for herself? Looked for the person — the girl — that someone else had seen?

Chapter 22

By two o'clock all that could be done toward having the reception ready was done. Finishing touches would have to wait until Mrs. Reed, Mrs. Armitage, Mrs. Monroe and Duncan hurried back from the church to get out the melon balls in wine, the meats and canapés, the salads and rolls and arrange them on the table, now beautiful on the back lawn.

Catty, from her window, looked down in wonder. In their Indiana town, wedding receptions had been catered because nobody had the time, and certainly nobody they knew had the house or grounds or possessions to give a lawn supper for nearly sixty. Here neighbors had driven up with family possessions, cheerfully offering for use Revere silver, Sandwich glass compotes, damask cloths, china.

Mrs. Armitage had declared herself breathtaken at the quality of things lent for the occasion. She was reverent in her handling and kept so sharp an eye on Duncan and Virginia and Catty, who had helped set up, that they became somewhat awed. Catty refused to touch anything but table silver, which she was pretty certain she wouldn't dent and knew she couldn't break.

"These cloths," said Mrs. Armitage, carefully smoothing pale pink damask over the board tables, "must be nearly a century old. See how they gleam. Considering their condition, I should say they've been very little used. You know, Marian Wendell, in her quiet way, utterly wins people's hearts. I'd be put to it to think of anyone else I know who would be given the loan of such linen. To say nothing of the rest of this — " She waved a hand at the tray of china Duncan was bearing, with wary circumspection, across the lawn.

"Two sets of china," Mrs. Monroe had pointed out. "One from the Bulls, and a set of Canton china that must have come over in the seventeenth century that belongs to Mr. Fell and his sister."

"It was a wedding present, I understand, to their great-great-grandmother, Retire Matheson — oh, those *names* — and the entire set was for one hundred, originally. Now it's down to approximately thirty, give or take a few soup tureens. He and his sister are the last of the line, and they—" She'd glanced about to be sure Marian and Mr. Grimmett were not within hearing "—

my dears, they are going to have it wrapped up when the reception is over and *present* it to Marian!"

Mrs. Monroe gasped. "My word! But it must be priceless."

"Indeed, yes. *Quelle geste!*" declared Mrs. Armitage.

Now, looking down at the almost completed reception arrangements, Catty thought the Canton china looked lovelier from up here. Close to, it was sort of busy, faintly grimy. From this distance it glowed like magic on the pink damask.

Mrs. Armitage had arranged, on the two long tables, centerpieces of tiny pink and white carnations and gypsophila. The wedding-cake table was unadorned save for the cloth. Mrs. Armitage and Mrs. Monroe said it only required the cake to grace that table.

And it only required, for the members of the wedding, to dress now and wait for cars that would take them to town, to the church, where Aunt Marian and John Grimmett would be married in the little side chapel in a ceremony so simple there hadn't even been a rehearsal.

But why, oh why, Catty implored Huck, who betrayed no interest, did her aunt choose to marry at four in the afternoon? A morning wedding, when everyone was fresh and taken—not unawares, of course—but on the crest, as it were, would have seen it over by now. Drive to the church, wedding ceremony, wedding breakfast, departure of the bride and groom, and now they could all be settling to familiar (or, in her case, entirely unfamiliar) roles.

Having the affair so late in the day had given everyone an opportunity to get keyed up, and some people, in particular Mrs. Charters, a chance to get hysterical because she was being neglected. She'd knocked a platter of sandwiches off the kitchen sideboard with her cane and then, instead of being abashed, had seemed all at once triumphantly tranquil. Poor Duncan, Catty had mourned, but he'd just grimaced and said, "The way I figure, Gram is stuck with that personality and she's doing the best she can with it. So'm I, of course. Stuck with it. But I expect we'll muddle through."

What Catty had wanted was to remain in the memory of those few early morning moments when she and Duncan had looked at each other and known something they hadn't known just before. She wanted to be alone in her room, to recall the sound of his voice, the expression on his dear face. How *could* a face, between one moment and the next, move into a person's heart so that the first sight of it was altogether lost? She could remember that at first she'd thought him handsome and then, for a while, had found him rather plain. Now she didn't know whether he was beautiful or not—only that that face had become the center of her being, that it was in her heart and in her mind. What she wanted was to be alone, remembering those moments and trying to believe them. Or no—she believed them—what she needed was to be alone to understand them.

But having promised Mrs. Armitage her help, she'd gone downstairs to breakfast, thinking Duncan would have left already for his classes, and there he was in the dining room, having breakfast with Mr. Fell.

Catty, unprepared, stood arrested in the doorway, a

flow of fire in her cheeks. She wanted to walk over and stand beside him and say, "Duncan, I love you, I am in love with you. Tell me that you love me, or will love me, tell me to live for you or run away with you or die for you—"

"Hello there, Catty," said Mr. Fell, cheerfully at ease, years and years past the danger of being caught in any such whirlpool as she was spinning in. "Get your gruel and join us, won't you?"

Duncan looked up, glanced away, said to the wainscoting, "Yes, join us, won't you?"

Did his voice sound unsteady? Did his hand holding the coffee cup tremble slightly? She didn't know, couldn't tell. She tried to smile in their direction, but could say nothing, and in the kitchen she leaned forward, hands on the wooden table, to catch her breath.

If this is being in love, she said to herself, I'm not sure I'll ever really take to it. At a sound, she turned, and there he stood, a tray of dishes in his hands, swallowing uneasily.

"Get these things put away," he said choppily. "Nobody else seems to be up yet. At least nobody's downstairs. Except Mr. Fell, of course. You saw him." He stood with his back to her, stacking the few dishes.

"I thought you'd be—that you'd be gone to your classes."

"Not going today. I have to—there are so many things—there's a lot to do today, so I—" He turned, clearing his throat. "Look, Catty, I think we'd better try to understand something—"

He's going to try to go back, she thought. To somehow undo something wonderful that's already been done.

"You're afraid of me, aren't you?" he said.

"No. Oh, no."

"Yes. You're afraid, and I did it to you, and it's a little hard to explain to a kid of your age —"

"I am not a kid, Duncan."

"You're a child. And I seem to be turning into a nineteen-year-old dirty old man."

"Stop!" She straightened and scowled at him. "Don't do that. Don't make something — something —" Her mouth and throat were so dry and scratchy. If she talked any more she'd choke, so she had, instead, to listen to him fumble his way into an explanation of how lovely she had looked in the early light, in her joy " — you seemed so marvelously happy. I've never seen anyone look so full of joy — so sort of primitive about it. I guess," he said, attempting a smile, "I had a kind of primitive reaction." He straightened. "Momentary, of course. Only momentary."

"Of course, Dunc." Catty's mouth drooped at the corners and her mind moved incoherently from wanting to go with his will, back to the way they'd been before their eyes met early in the morning as if their eyes had never met before — which, in a sense, they had not — and wanting to reach out and touch his face, lean forward and put her lips on his. What if I said, "I'm in love with you, Duncan. It only took a moment for me to know, but now I know"? She permitted herself a sigh, as if she'd already had his answer. "You can't be in love, Catty. Anyway, not with me. You're only thirteen."

But I can be, she told him wordlessly. I can be. I am.

Enough to pretend not, since that's how you need it to be. She smiled at him sadly. "You don't have to explain so much, you know. It was perfectly lovely, but not such a big deal, dear Duncan."

He regarded her with a mixture of relief, tenderness, and — just possibly? — regret.

"Well then," he said. "Okay. Have to get those boards up on the sawhorses. Promised Mrs. A. I'd get at those first thing. See you, Cats."

He was gone, out of the kitchen to the open world. Catty, looking after him, realized that only yesterday she'd have trotted right on after him to help. Now she turned, and went looking for Mrs. Armitage, or Mrs. Monroe — someone who'd give her a task to perform, here in the house.

A long time later she was dressed and sitting in her room, in the little wing chair, strangely out of spirits, when Virginia came up to get her.

"Come along, Catty. The cars are ready. Why are you glooming here alone?"

Catty looked up. "How pretty you look, Ginny. I guess I mean beautiful."

"Well, that's nice," Virginia said confidently. "But I asked about you. What's wrong? You *look* very nice. Darling, actually. The curls are a success."

In one of her sweet moods, that could be very sweet. Maybe, Catty thought, she'll have them more often as she ripens to maturity. Maybe we'll get to be close after all, and then I could tell her that I'm tired, that I'm sad, that I'm in love and confused.

Not yet, though.

187

"I just feel tired. I don't know why."

"Too much going on. Besides, it's physiological," Ginny said with assurance. "People of your age are going through all sorts of exhausting physical changes. I well remember how it felt. All that business can be traumatic for a girl, and *very* tiring."

"Is that so?"

"It is. I've read all about it. You'll just have to expect these downs and make up your mind that's all they are. Temporary downs that come from being your age and living in our age. Nothing soothing about either one, but you'll pull through because everybody does."

Not everybody, thought Catty, but would not disagree with her sister now in this extraordinary moment of sympathy.

"Well, shall we go?" said Ginger. "Wait until you *see* the nasturtium hat. Sheer poetry. I'd never have thought Mrs. Monroe had it in her. I'll tell you something, Catty — the world is *full* of startling surprises. That's what makes it so much fun. Let's *go*."

Chapter 23

Mrs. John Grimmett said to her niece, Catty, "Darling, of course I invited him. You know how he is. *I* couldn't tell from the way he reacted whether he wanted to go to the wedding or not, and I guess I sort of assumed he wouldn't. Isn't that what anyone would assume?"

Aunt Marian, cheeks flushed, eyes glowing, was attempting to mind terribly that Mr. Hermann had missed the wedding. Because she was fond of Catty, because this was her day and John's and they were married and she wanted her happiness to embrace everyone, she tried to take a moment to care how Mr. Hermann was feeling.

But, really, it was too difficult. Someone came up to her, arms out, proclaiming her beauty, the beauty of the ceremony, the beauty of the day and the buffet and the gardens and that *master*piece of a cake I understand Henry actually did it all him*self*—and without in the least meaning to Mrs. Grimmett forgot Catty and Mr. Hermann utterly.

Catty looked around the crowded lawn. Family and guests were seated at the prettily arranged bridge tables, eating, talking, laughing, and always circling around Aunt Marian and John, who were now married to each other and though still at the inn, no longer part of it.

The best man had proposed a charming and, Catty thought, not altogether appropriate toast. Something about the sun always shining on them gently and the rain always falling on their fields and God holding them in the palm of his hand, and champagne had been drunk and the wedding cake cut, and one could feel Aunt Marian, Mrs. Grimmett, gone from here in spirit toward her new home in the West, and undoubtedly in just a little while she'd be gone in fact.

So now, thought Catty, nibbling a canapé — she found she couldn't eat a real supper — now we are the inn-keepers. Us and Uncle Henry.

When they'd all got back from the church late this afternoon, there had been, among the telegrams of congratulation, a wire for her father asking him to get in touch with his boss. His erstwhile boss.

Mr. Reed had called his family upstairs, to his room, to show it to them.

"What are you going to do about it?" his wife asked.

"Call him, naturally. Not today. In the morning."

"What if he's offering you your job back, or another job someplace else?"

"That's why I asked you all up here. What if he is? It seems it ought to be sort of a family decision. Not just mine alone. What do you think, Amy?"

She looked at him closely and said, "I don't want to sound quaint, but just the same — I want what you want. Whatever you feel is best for you."

"And you children?" he asked. "What are your ideas?"

Virginia, after a pause, said, "Wouldn't leaving now be sort of hard on Uncle Henry? I mean, as Mom says, you're the one who must do what's best for you. But I was just wondering — "

"I thought you resented being here, Ginger."

Virginia lifted delicate shoulders. "I won't be here forever. There's school, and college, and — whatever comes then. And in the meantime — well, in the meantime I don't resent it anymore. Parts of it I sort of like."

Like all those young men in the wedding party, Catty thought, grateful to Aunt Marian's friend, who had produced them.

"I love it here!" Lexy burst out.

"That's not the point," Ginny began. "The point is whether Daddy wants to stay or go."

"No," said Mr. Reed. "Whether you children can be happy here *is* the point. Because your mother and I know where we stand." He looked at his wife who smiled and said, oh yes, they knew and had known for ages.

"Where's that?" said Catty.

"Here. In this decent, modest, human job that can in no way contribute to human suffering or indignity. If that sounds stuffy, there's no help for it, it's still the truth. I don't want to go back to helping society devise ways and means of destroying itself. Your mother and I want to live here, traveling widely in northeast Vermont, and help Uncle Henry run his inn. We want to learn how to walk on snowshoes come winter. That's as far as our ambition takes us anymore. So — what about you, Catty?"

"My heart's here. All over the place," she added.

And so it was settled. They, with Uncle Henry, were the innkeepers. Therefore the guests were their responsibility. Therefore the matter of Mr. Hermann must be taken care of.

A most peculiar man, Mr. Hermann. He didn't smile oftener than an aloe bloomed, he didn't talk with people or uncover his feelings in any way, and yet he had come, walking the two miles to the church in the heat, jacket carefully folded over his arm, because they'd all quite simply forgotten him as they got into cars for the drive to the church. He'd arrived as everyone was waiting at the chapel doors for Mr. and Mrs. Grimmett to emerge, and he'd gotten a little shower of rice straight in his face. He'd been offered a ride home, which he accepted with a slow nod, and did not attend the reception but retired immediately to his room.

Which, Catty said to herself now, means that he's foregone supper altogether. And he hadn't had any dinner, because there hadn't been any dinner that day. Just snatched sandwiches and milk and coffee. She hadn't seen him around for those.

Last week, yesterday even, Aunt Marian, with her ever-alert sensitivity to the old people's needs, would

have noticed this and done something about it. Today —
well today, Catty said to herself, he's *ours* to see to.

I'll tell Ginny, she thought. Ginny always knows what
to do about old people.

The little band was playing, and as the bride and
groom had had their turn about the dance floor, others
were now crowded upon it, and the others were mostly
young. Aunt Marian's friend in the English department
at the college, hearing that a lovely young girl was at
the inn and hadn't yet met any people her own age, had
provided the wedding party with a dozen students of
assorted sex, mostly male. And these boys, like other
men and boys, on first sight of Virginia had widened
their eyes and started forward as if pulled on strings.
She'd been dancing or sitting out dances in a circle of
admirers like Scarlett O'Hara ever since.

She was dancing now with Duncan, and Catty couldn't
bring herself to interrupt. Duncan, as the day progressed,
had drawn more and more into the protection of his six
years seniority, as if in that way he could undo, or forget,
something that, if it hadn't been such a big deal, had
certainly been a sweet deal.

Catty turned from the dance floor and went looking
for her parents. She'd tell them that Mr. Hermann was
up in his room, alone and undoubtedly hungry. Or she'd
find Uncle Henry, and —

Oh, for heaven's sakes, she thought, and went to get
a tray. Walking along the buffet tables, she selected a
proper supper for an old gentleman who'd fasted most
of the day, including a piece of wedding cake on which
she carefully placed a candied rose. In the kitchen she

filled a little pot with coffee and then went firmly up-stairs and knocked on Mr. Hermann's door.

While she waited for him to answer, she looked down the open staircase to the hall where the nine-foot grand-father clock was striking seven.

Home, she thought, smiling.

After she gave Mr. Hermann his tray, she'd go down and ask Duncan to dance, even if she had to cut in on Virginia.